Songstrom

Simon Birks

Songström

First Edition

First Published in the UK by Blue Fox Publishing Limited
Copyright 2017 © Simon Birks

Visit **http://bluefoxcomics.com** to read more about all our books,
comics and other publications.

For Marielle,
For holding the torch
when I run out of hands.

It started with a phone call I couldn't remember.

Songström

Freya and I had spoken about Songström before. In the dark of the night I would whisper to her about it, describe how it looked, what lived inside. I'd tell her I hated it, that I never wanted to go back. I told her to keep away.

When the sun rose, however, when the morning came, she'd deny I'd ever said a thing. She'd look at me, unable to speak.

We lived an existence together, but sometimes we were so very much apart. Sometimes, I had to remind myself we were actually a couple at all.

Bobby didn't want to talk about Freya. Bobby just wanted to talk about whatever it was he'd done that day and that was fine. Bobby was a good friend; my only friend, apart from Freya.

*

1

The day the end came for me, for Bobby, for Freya, had been like any other day. I went to work at the supermarket, on the day shift, which I liked because it meant I could meet Freya for coffee at lunchtime.

The morning had dragged. I couldn't focus on just one job; I had to keep moving around the store to avoid the management. Lately, they'd been arguing with me a lot, and whilst I didn't like it, I could put up with it. I was about to clock off for lunch, when Bobby called me over. He worked on the floor, talking to the customers.

"Look at this," he said, and indicated a television. "Looks fucking good, doesn't it?"

Bobby swears a lot. It's a shame, but it's also who he is. Bobby is not like me.

The television was indeed impressive in size. It was currently showing an underwater scene from a movie I didn't recognise. I nodded to him.

"Looks okay," I said.

"Doesn't anything make you fucking happy?" Bobby asked.

"You do," I told him.

"Yeah, yeah," he said. Bobby wandered off, muttering, towards a woman looking at some new mobile phones.

I looked at the picture again. There was something worrying about the water.

*

When I got to the café, Freya seemed anxious. I noted she hadn't ordered anything.

"Everything all right?" I asked her.

"Listen, Sammel," she said, unusually aggressive. "Just listen. I need to tell you about this, and you need to take it in, got it?" She tapped me gently on the head. "It needs to get in there and stick. It's really important. Got it?"

"Got it," I nodded. The tapping didn't hurt, but it was embarrassing. The café was opposite the supermarket, a place we regularly met. The staff knew me. Served me. Smiled at me. I didn't want them thinking I was stupid, or forgetful, however stupid or forgetful I was.

"Look at this," Freya was saying, as she fiddled with her handbag. Freya carried everything in her handbag. I didn't know how she did it.

"Can't we talk about this at home?" I asked, but she pretended not to hear.

"It's in here somewhere," she said. Her voice was starting to rise, which meant she wasn't far off tipping the whole bag upside down onto the table.

"What is it? Perhaps I could look for it?" I asked. The waiter brought my coffee over and put it on the table. "Thank you," I said.

"Here, here it is."

She removed a spectacle case from her bag. It was battered, the black leather covering coming apart at the edges. She put it on the table.

"This is the box which sits on the shelf in our room. The one you told me never to open," I said to her.

"That's correct. Today you can open it."

I didn't move. "Why? What's different about today?"

"Just open it."

I looked at her face, trying to work out exactly what the contents might be.

"Open it," she said, slowly and deliberately. Her gaze somehow intensified. I felt under pressure.

Then I smiled. I realised she was excited, and I couldn't remember the last time she'd been excited. I reached forward and put my hands on the case.

"Is this going to be weird?" I asked.

"Of course."

I found the seam where the case opened and put my fingernails into it, twisting as I did so. It was unlikely to be anything nasty, but, at the same time, I wasn't going to take any chances.

I lifted the top a little and peered into the darkness within. Something was shining in there. I pushed the topmost part of the case fully open, revealing a cube of dark stone, about an inch wide on each side. I couldn't be sure, but I thought it might be Onyx.

I looked at Freya, confused. She looked at me, down to the cube, and then back up at me.

"What is it?" I asked, and even before I'd finished, her hands had darted out and plucked the cube from the case, removing it from the square recess it had been slotted into.

"This is Sikkilite," she said. "Have you ever seen it before?"

I shook my head.

"It's very pretty," I said, but I was just being nice. In truth, it was no worse nor better than any other polished stone I'd ever seen.

"It doesn't matter whether it's pretty or not," she said, her eyes shining. "That's not why we've got it."

She was being secretive, but only because she wanted me to ask more questions. I was happy to play along. "Why have we got it?"

"Because," she started, leaning in closer. "When we die, it keeps our souls intact."

I waited to see if she'd say any more, to see if she'd elaborate on such a bold claim. She didn't.

"Well," I told her. "I really don't know what to say."

Freya laughed, a tinkling sound, too young for her years. "Isn't it exciting?" she asked.

I nodded. "I suppose so. Why haven't you showed me this before?"

A different smile then. A fleeting, sad smile, alien to a face like Freya's. It was gone in a moment, and left her with a serious look.

"Do I need a reason?" she asked. "I thought you'd be happy I showed it to you."

"I am," I said, trying to soothe her. "I'm very pleased. I was just wondering if I'd done something right, that's all."

"No," she said. "It was just the right time to show you."

A faraway look stole over her; she was going off the boil now, her excitement spent in those too few minutes. If I wanted to get any more information from her, I'd have to try and make her focus.

"Where did you get it from?"

Freya put the Sikkilite back into the case and shut the lid.

"Oh, I found it," she said. She stirred her coffee in silence.

"Where did you find it?"

"It doesn't matter where I found it, or what it looks like, or that you never help me. All that matters is what it's able to do, Sammel."

I wasn't sure what she meant about never helping her. I'm a very helpful person. Very tidy, as well, but she was upset, and I didn't think asking for an explanation would help remedy the situation.

"May I take another look at it?" I asked. "At the Sikkilite?"

She looked at me then, and a smile turned up the very corners of her mouth. "You remembered its name," she said, reaching over and touching my cheek.

"You asked me to remember. You said it was important."

"Remembering is important, Sammel," she said with a sigh, which sounded very close to a yawn. She pushed the case over to me, and withdrew her hands.

I opened it once more. "May I take it out?" I asked.

Freya nodded with little conviction. Her mood appeared to be changing from moment to moment. I didn't like it when people did that. I liked knowing how people are going to act. I wanted to ask her to stop doing it. I wanted to tell her to grow up. I didn't. I don't say a lot of things I want to say.

I reached in and took the black stone out. There was a hole through the centre that I hadn't noticed earlier. "What's this for?" I asked.

Freya reached over to the case, lifted up the piece of crimson velvet lining the inside of the box, and removed a brown leather string. "It's to put this through," she said. "You have to wear it like a necklace."

"I see. And how does it keep your soul intact?"

Freya shrugged. "I don't know," she said, another laugh in her voice. "It just does. I don't question it. When you've been round as long as I have, Sammel, you accept that some things just are."

Some things just are. I thought about that for a moment. In truth, I reasoned, everything just was. Otherwise, it wouldn't be anything. It would be nothing. I looked around myself, and tried to picture being surrounded by nothing, by four white walls. I thought it might make me feel safe, but it didn't. It just made me feel alone.

I came back to the café.

"I'm not sure any of this makes sense," I told her.

If she heard me, she made no effort to reply. "I like this café," she said. "It's where we met. I like the windows, so big and they let so much light through. It reminds me of fire. Do you remember the fire, Sammel? I loved you from the moment I saw you, and I saw you before you saw me, so I've loved you the longest."

"I don't remember a fire," I told her.

"But I saw you through it and you were so beautiful; alone, and so wise. There's nothing about you that I couldn't love. And I never believed it would be possible. But I saw you and I knew it, and I thought, now there's a man that could save me. And that's why I came to you and asked for your help. That's why I showed you the Sikkilite."

"I'm not sure what you're saying."

Freya took the Sikkilite from me and threaded the leather necklace through. She placed it around her neck. "Would you?" she asked, half turning so I could see the two ends in her hands. I stood and stepped next to her.

"There isn't going to be a lot of room for the knot," I told her.

"That's okay," she replied. "It needs to be nice and tight."

"If that's what you want," I said. It took me three attempts to successfully tie the ends together.

"Thank you," she whispered, as I sat back down.

"Can you breathe okay?" I asked her. The black cube was digging into her neck.

She nodded. "It's... okay. It has to be okay."

I looked at my shoes. They were brogues with longer laces. "Let me use one of these," I said, but Freya was already shaking her head.

"You don't understand," she said. "You won't understand. But you need to understand. And it needs to be you who understands."

"But..." I started, then looked around the café, and decided not to pursue it. I'd try and convince her when we were at home.

"How long do you have to wear it?"

"For the rest of my life."

I almost laughed, and would have, if the look on her face hadn't been so serious. "The rest of your life?"

"It's okay," Freya replied. "Everything's going to be okay."

She looked at her watch. "Lunch is over. I have to go." She picked up her bag.

I tried to grab her hand, but missed. "Where do you want to meet tonight?" I called after her.

"I'll message you," she said.

"I miss you," I said. She stopped.

"I miss you, too," she said, but it sounded different, like the Sikkilite was making it hard to say the words. Or like she was crying. She didn't turn around, and she left.

*

I didn't go back to the supermarket that afternoon. Instead I walked. I wanted to walk. Wanted to clear my head. The encounter with Freya in the café had been confusing. I had wanted it to be clear, I had wanted an easy exchange of communication, but I hadn't got it. It had thrown me. I needed to walk.

I chose the hills. I could have chosen the roads, or the beach, but the hills seemed right. It was a good walk, too. I wasn't worried about distance or time. I just wanted to plant my feet on the ground, wanted to feel that connection.

I knew Freya was odd, like I knew I was odd. Being odd was just being normal in your own way. Freya and I got on well. It was easy to be with her, and she told me she felt the same. I had been committed to her from our first meeting, though exactly when that first meeting had occurred, was lost to me.

When I'd walked enough, when I felt calm again, I found another café and sat with a cup of tea. At times, I was the only person there, which was fine by me. I'm used to that. At four o'clock, I looked at my phone and realised it was off. I hadn't turned it on since lunch. I thought about turning it on, but it was another hour at least until Freya would leave work, so there wouldn't be anyone to talk to.

I didn't have anywhere to be, and I doubted the supermarket had even missed me. I left the phone off. Everyone could wait.

*

I knew I'd outstayed my meagre custom when the owner of the café began shuffling chairs noisily for no particular reason. I smiled, paid the bill and left. I didn't like it. I'd been happy there.

Walking back, my legs were stiff, which slowed my pace. It'd been a while since I'd had such a long walk. I guess that's what happens. Your circles get smaller all the time, until one day you realise you're hardly moving at all.

I made it back to our flat at five forty-two. I know this because that was when I turned my phone back on. I climbed the stairs, waiting for a message from Freya to pop up, but nothing came through. It wasn't unusual.

*

I ran the shower and the water was hot. I might have spent too long in there, but it didn't matter. I was warm, and the water was a welcome distraction from the thoughts in my head. When I finished, I drew the shower curtain back. The room beyond was mostly mist, swirling patterns that caught my eye.

I didn't get straight out, which is what I normally did. I waited. Something was different; the darkness of the room seemed bigger.

"Hello?" I asked.

My voice echoed, and I knew it wasn't the bathroom at all. I was somewhere else, somewhere vast, and damp. I didn't like it, but not wholly. Part of me was intrigued. A dangerous part of me needed to be here, to be in jeopardy, because everyday life had become too tedious.

I looked to where the ceiling should be, and saw nothing but darkness stretching away. It took my eyes a moment to adjust, but when they had, I could make out a subtle change in colour, further up, a deep blueness that could have been the midnight sky.

"Hello?" I called once more into the mist. It sucked the words in, dampened them, saturated them, until they were little more than vibrations in water. "My name is Sammel. Sammel Ahlberg."

I imagined the water moving, imagined the speech coming out of my mouth like actual letters and words, spinning through the mist, pushing it aside on their quest for someone to listen to them.

"I know who you are," came a reply. It was a female voice. Sarcastic. Angry. "What are you doing here?"

I picked up my towel and put it around me. "Well, you're in my bathroom. I didn't have a choice."

"There will always be a choice, Sammel," the woman mocked.

I stepped out of the bath. "Do I know you?"

"Leave me alone," she replied, a nervousness to her voice. "I'm happy here."

I took a step closer. "Where is here?"

12

A pause. She was thinking.

"Here is a space where my brain doesn't need to lie. Nothing is expected of me, and I expect nothing of anyone else."

"Do you know where Freya is?" I asked.

She laughed then. "Sammel and Freya sitting in the sea... M. I. S. S. I. N. G." She sang this with childish hatred.

I took another step. "Where is she?"

"I'm not going to tell you, Sammel Ahlberg. But I will do something."

"What?"

"Let me leave you a clue." There was a pause. "There. It's done."

I took another step forward, and my foot hit the bathroom door. I blinked and I was back in the flat. I checked the ceiling. The midnight sky had gone. Part of me was happy. Part of me wasn't.

I towelled myself dry and went into the hallway.

"Freya?" I called, but I could tell by the echo she still wasn't home. What sort of clue had the woman left?

My phone was on the bed, so I went and checked it. No messages. I rang Freya's number, but it didn't connect. It does that. Sometimes the reception isn't good. I rang again as I dressed in jeans and a shirt. Nothing. I rang five more times as I prepared a snack for myself; tuna on toast, all with the same result.

I ate the food at the table, waiting for a reply. Why couldn't I reach her? Had I upset her at the café earlier? She usually forgave me, at

13

least that's what I thought. She usually said that however wrong I'd been, everything was okay again.

I remembered the woman in the bathroom saying she'd left a clue, but I couldn't see one in the lounge. Sometimes I wanted to do things, really wanted to do them, but I couldn't be bothered to get up. That was how I felt, now. I thought I wanted to find Freya, but what I actually wanted was for her to turn up, and for everything to be as it was before the Sikkilite episode.

Perhaps Bobby would help me. I looked at my phone, and remembered I didn't have his number. Even if I did, he'd probably just tell me to get myself straight. He wouldn't want to talk about Freya. He'd say she was my own 'shit' that I needed to sort out.

*

I made some tea and waited, hoping for the phone to ring. Halfway through my second cup, it did.

"Hello?"

"Is this Sammel Ahlberg?"

"Yes. I'm Sammel."

"This is Constable Jackson, from the police station. You rang and left a message."

"Did I?"

"Yes, you reported your girlfriend missing." I didn't remember doing this, but sometimes I do things without realising it.

"Oh, right. Do you have some information?"

14

"There's been a handbag left at the train station. By the look of the contents, it belongs to a woman named Freya. That's your girlfriend's name, isn't it?"

"Yes, it is. Right, should I come and collect it?"

"That's why I'm ringing. I thought you might like it."

"Yes. Yes I would."

It was a clue. The clue. The woman in the mist had helped me, after all.

I didn't have a car, and Bobby never drove, so I took my bicycle. The police station wasn't far away, and I rode as quickly as I could.

I couldn't remember going to the police station before. I couldn't picture the inside of it. That's how I generally remember places, I take a mental picture when I'm there. Just a snippet, and when later I try to recall what it looked like, I build everything around that snippet. I'd read about fractals on the internet, and that's what I likened the process to.

*

I liked this town. It wasn't my home town. My home town was in another country, but it was my adopted town, and we got on well.

It wasn't very big, not very crowded, and I found myself riding in that strange time of day, when the work traffic had all but gone, and the evening revellers hadn't yet ventured out into the cold.

When I arrived, I walked up the steps, locked my bike to the railings outside, and pushed open the heavy front door. I checked my watch; it was eight twenty-two.

"Hello," I called out to the empty reception area. The room was sparse with a smattering of posters on the magnolia painted walls. "Hello?"

There was a noise of something being knocked over, followed by someone muttering "Shit," under their breath.

"One moment," the voice called.

"No rush," I said, though it sounded odd. I was in a rush. I wanted to find Freya.

The man appeared in civilian clothes. "Hello," he said.

"I'm Sammel Ahlberg. You rang me about my girlfriend's handbag?"

He looked at me, appraising me before speaking. "That's right. Nice to meet you, Sammel. I'm Constable Jackson." He offered his hand, and I shook it.

"I'm surprised you're open so late."

"Friday is late night opening," he said, with a twinkle in his eye. "If there's any trouble in this town, Friday is the night it'll start. It's sad, but then, that's what I'm here for. I'm supposing you want the bag?" he asked.

"Yes, please."

"Before I give it to you, I'll need a form of ID. Did I tell you that on the phone? I don't believe I did. I'm sorry about that. You definitely need a form of ID."

"No problem," I told him. "I thought I might." I put my hand into my jacket pocket and brought out my passport. Constable Jackson took it and looked at it for a moment, flicking through the pages.

"I'll need to take a copy of this," he said, and left before I could reply.

*

I waited a few moments, and when he didn't return, decided to look at the posters. I supposed that that was what they were there for. The first told cyclists to lock their bicycles, and that made me smile. Smile, and turn and check my bicycle was still there.

The next informed children about stranger danger. It was a cartoon drawing showing an adult offering a child some sweets. Stranger danger wasn't a phrase when I was young. I was just told not to talk to any strange people. It struck me that Constable Jackson was a strange person, but I had to talk to him.

The final poster was about the neighbourhood watch scheme. There was a group of people shown, with a policeman smiling at the centre of them. We didn't have neighbourhood watch at the flats. It was everyone for themselves there.

I'd wanted to use one of the posters to remember the police station, but, in truth, I didn't think I could. I didn't like them. None of them made any sense. They didn't say fear, and fear seemed to be at the centre of all of them.

*

I walked back to the counter and checked my phone again. Nothing. Without warning, an anxiousness unfolded in my chest, and tried to smother me. Was I being silly about all of this? Perhaps Freya had just had to stay late at work. Or perhaps the car had broken down, or she needed to pick some shopping up.

I looked towards the door, towards my bicycle chained up outside. I wanted to leave. I wanted to run and hide. Freya would come back, of course she would. Freya's never been away before. She's just a little late and I've over-thought it.

Then a coldness. A smoothness. New questions appeared. What about the Sikkilite? What about the bathroom, which hadn't been a bathroom, and the woman who'd spoken to me?

There was a noise, and Constable Jackson appeared with my passport and Freya's bag.

"Thank you," he said, placing the bag on the table and putting the passport in the bag. "You're not originally from here?"

"No, I moved here when I was younger," I said.

"With your parents?" he asked. It seemed like a strange question. I remembered watching police television shows with my father when I was younger. This was the line of questioning they might take.

Obscure, confusing, and then, at the last minute, they'd ask the question they'd been wanting to ask all along.

"No," I said.

Constable Jackson smiled. He seemed to have gotten the answer he'd wanted. "Please contact us tomorrow, Sammel, if you haven't heard anything, or even if you have. It'd be nice to know where she is."

"Okay."

"In the meantime, I suggest you wait at home. She's probably there, even now."

"Thank you, Officer," I said. We shook hands. He smiled, nodded, and watched me leave.

*

Outside the police station, I checked the time again. It was eight fifty. It had been almost eight hours since I'd last seen Freya. I opened my wallet and looked at the picture of her I kept in there. Yes, she was just how I remembered her. I touched the photo, traced the outline of her jaw with my index finger. She was beautiful. I would like nothing more than to arrive home and see her waiting for me.

I unlocked the chain securing the bicycle, dropped it into my rucksack, and mounted the saddle. I paused, and looked back through the glass door of the police station.

Constable Jackson was just the other side of the door, staring at me, head cocked to one side. There was something hungry about his look, about his stance. I jerked backwards, lost my balance, and fell, the bicycle landing on my leg. The back of my head cracked against the railings, and for a few moments, my vision was filled with flashing lights.

The police station door opened, and I tried to focus.

"Is everything okay?" Jackson said. "I saw you fall."

"Er, yes," I stammered. "Everything's just fine. I thought... I just got disorientated."

I felt Jackson's hand close around my arm and he helped me up.

"I expect you're feeling stressed about Freya," he said.

"Yes, it must be. Thank you for coming to help."

"I'm a policeman. That's what we do." He picked up my bike, brushed the saddle, and held it upright. I began to climb on. "Perhaps you should push it home."

"I'm okay," I told him.

"I think you need some rest, Sammel. You look tired."

"Thank you again," I said, wanting to leave. I checked over the gears and the brakes, everything looked fine. I pushed myself off and started to ride away.

"Good luck," Jackson said. I waved over my shoulder, but didn't look around.

*

It took me longer to cycle home from the police station. I stopped a couple of times, and breathed deeply until I had my nerves back under control. It was difficult to forget the image of Jackson standing so near to the door, looking so strange. There had been something about his face, something that I should remember, but couldn't. Like my mind was hiding it from me, keeping me safe.

My flat came into view, and my heart sank. It was still in darkness. Freya wasn't home.

*

When I was younger, I loved forests. I loved exploring them, finding different ways through them. It was an obsession, of sorts. I don't know what drove it. Many times, I'd think I was hopelessly lost, and it would scare me so much I'd panic, and run.

This was how I found Songström; how I found the place I would never forget.

I can't remember exactly how I got there. One minute I was in trees, the next I was in the centre of three huts, each standing on identical concrete cones with wooden steps leading up to their entrances. Two of the huts were run down. One had a hole in the roof, another had a door that was mostly detached. The third one, like the chair in Goldilocks, appeared just right.

They looked both ordinary and extraordinary. Nothing about them frightened me, though there was something wrong in the stillness they inhabited. I could have walked away. I could have walked away and not known Songström. I think my life would have been different if I had. Not normal, just different.

I went to the hut with the broken door first, gingerly testing each step with my foot before trusting it with the rest of my weight. Not that I was overweight back then. In fact, as far as I can remember, I was a very thin child. It was just that the boards seemed rotten at the edges, and I didn't know how far the rot had set in.

There was a gap between the framework and the tilted door, large enough for me to see through into the hut's interior. Mostly it was dark, with a smell of damp wood, and perhaps something far more pungent lurking underneath. There was a feeling, too. Regret, maybe. Or guilt.

The next hut, the one with the hole in the roof, was lighter inside. It had a simple layout, with a seating area to the left, and kitchen to the right. Beside the kitchen, a door led off to what I guessed would be the toilet. I couldn't see any other doors. I briefly wondered if it had a bedroom at all.

The third hut looked sturdier. I went up these steps with more confidence, stopping at the door. There was a plaque by it, weathered, but readable. It read 'Songström'. I'd never heard of it.

I knocked on the door. This surprised me. I'd convinced myself I'd simply grip the handle, twist, and walk straight in, unannounced. Now that I was here, however, I thought that would be rude. It wasn't what the hut deserved.

I waited for a moment. When no answer came, I opened the door and stepped inside.

The air smelled fresh, varnished, and polished.

"Hello," I said.

It was the same layout as the other hut. There was a coffee table that came up to my knees in front of the sofa, and in front of that, an unlit log fire sat shiny and spotless. The kitchen area was similarly clean, the cupboards and drawers empty of any objects.

I went to the sofa and sat on it. It was soft like a bed. At one end was a cushion with an embroidered picture of a steam train passing through trees. I liked the picture. I liked trains. I felt safe in this strange place, safe and tired. I put the cushion flat on the sofa, lifted my legs and lay down.

I twisted onto my back, and faced the roof above me. It had steeple-like wooden sides, which met in the middle, and something about their geometry made me yawn. I felt my eyes starting to close, and knew I could do nothing about it.

*

I felt the wind on my face, and my eyes snapped open.

I was standing on the hut with the hole in the roof, looking down into the blackness below. There was something moving in there. Something dark and large. It kept to the edges; it was the edges. I wanted to back away, but I was frightened I'd slip. The thing inside looked up and saw me, recognised me.

23

"I'm coming," it breathed, and began to rise.

I had to escape, whatever the risk of falling. I turned my body to flee, but my feet didn't move. I looked down, to where the roof tiles should be, but saw only hundreds of blackened arms reaching up, hands wide and clutching. Some of them, the nearest ones, held my legs. I wanted to scream, but knew that was what the shadow wanted. It wanted me to be scared. It had led me here, and it wanted to consume me.

The swarm of limbs clawed and grabbed at my legs. I tried to stop the panic growing in my mind. This was a madness. There would be a way out; there must be. If I stood upright for long enough, I would survive.

One of the arms, smaller and younger than the others, started pressing its fingernails into my flesh, harder and harder. It was agony, and I wanted to cry out, wanted my parents there, no matter how much they argued.

"Leave me alone," I said. "Leave me alone!"

I tried to shake myself free, and watched the fingernails of the young hand break the surface of my skin. My blood oozed out, throbbed down my leg, and into the sea of arms.

The black mass, which had been inside the hut, was now covering the hole in the roof. It had reached me, and nothing stood in its way.

"Let go!" I screamed. "Let me go!"

The hands disappeared, and I was caught off balance. I fell forwards, towards the all-consuming darkness, watching in horror as it took over all my vision. There was nothing I could do. Instinctively, I threw my arms forward.

Time slowed down, or at least my perception of it did. My hands met the blackness, and as they did, my fingers became dust, blown away on the wind. It was as much fascinating as it was horrific. I was disintegrating. Soon, there would be no more Sammel. I was going to die, and no one would ever find me. I would disappear below the surface of the world, and that would be that.

"No," I said, quietly, and sadly.

*

I jolted awake on the sofa in the hut, panicked but alive. I was on my side, and could see the gleaming fireplace. I was relieved. I had never had a dream so terrifying. The darkness; I didn't dare shut my eyes in case it had found a place to live in there.

The cushion below my head moved. There was something different about its shape. It no longer felt like a cushion. Instead, it was harder, and there was a dip in the middle. I gasped. My head was resting on someone's lap.

"There, there," came a woman's voice. "It was all just a bad dream."

I wanted to get up, to roll off, but her hand gripped my arm and prevented me from moving.

"Let me go," I groaned.

"Not just yet," she whispered. Her hand started to stroke my hair, and it was an old hand. It smelt of smoke, of blood and shit all at the same time. "I'm in need of you."

"Who... who are you?" I asked.

"I am the woman who is holding you," she said. "And who are you?"

"Sammel. Sammel Ahlberg," I sputtered. It felt like I was going to be sick.

"Well, Sammel, didn't anyone teach you not to go into other people's houses?"

"Yes."

"But still you came. You should have helped her, it was the right thing to do. Instead, you came here. Into my house. So, it's all your fault, isn't it? Your fault you're trapped here. Your fault you'll never escape."

I shook my head. Her grip became tighter.

"It is," she continued. "Now, I just need to hear you say it. It's your fault, Sammel. It's all your fault. Say it."

"No."

"Say it, or I'll scoop out your brain and eat it whilst you watch."

"No!"

"I warned you."

She shifted forward, leaning closer to me, and something dropped onto my skin. I thought it might be saliva, or worse, blood. Then it began to wriggle on my cheek. Repulsed, I shook my head, and it fell to the floor below. A maggot. Plump and white, that, until recently, had been gorging on this woman's face.

I was sick. Hot liquid squirted out of my mouth as I brought up that morning's breakfast. The woman recoiled, her grip loosening a fraction. It was enough. I threw my body forward and rolled off the couch, listening to her scream. I was pleased for it. She should scream, I thought. She should scream until her throat bled.

She grasped for my hair, her thin fingers trying to get a piece of me, but failing. My hands landed in the vomit, became slimy with it, and for a split-second I thought I wasn't going to be able to get away. Then I felt the edge of the rug on the floor, and took a hold of it. My right foot found the other end of the sofa, and between the two I managed to scuttle backwards.

I was clear of the sofa, of the maggot woman, but I was far from safe. If I could get out of the house, she wouldn't be able to follow. I knew this, like I knew my own name.

I couldn't look at her. If I saw her face then she would have me; she would torture me, forever. I stood, my gaze stuck fast to the floor, turned, and jumped. I covered the distance in one leap. A surge of hope ran through me. My hands grabbed at the cool, smooth handle and twisted. It was difficult. The vomit was making gripping harder, but the terror within me gave me strength. The handle moved and the door opened, the air outside rushing in as I ran through, into it, pulling the door closed behind me, making sure I heard the click.

Something hit the inside of the door.

I turned back then, to check it was securely closed. It was, but my eyes fell on the sign, which read Songström, and it became my warning. The word that would embody fear, for I had no other word that could define the terror I'd just felt.

There was a movement by the window to the left of the door, behind the yellowed net curtains. They moved, and a hand - her hand - pressed against the glass. I watched, against my will, as the palm lifted off the window, leaving a smear, and then pointed at me with one finger, the nail black.

"I have need of you," I heard her say in my head. "You are already mine."

I returned my own one-finger gesture, although my hand was shaking, and ran.

*

I was never sure Songström existed. In the days following that initial encounter, it took on a surreal, otherworldly tone. It was probably my brain trying to come to terms with everything, and that was all right. My brain was looking out for me, after all.

I can't say it didn't affect me, however. I was different after it. My parents, when they weren't arguing, grew concerned, and then watchful, and finally accepting. By the time I'd moved to this town, they were lost to me, and I was alone in the forest, again.

*

The carpet on the stairs up to my flat was almost threadbare, and as I climbed them, I wondered what exactly I was paying the maintenance money for.

On the first-floor landing, a man I often saw was waiting for me to pass. I'd attempted smiling at him once, a while ago, but he didn't seem to like smiling. He had a full beard, black with some flecks of white. The name on his jacket said 'Teddy', but I wasn't sure if that was his name, the make of the jacket, or even just the company he worked for.

I smiled at him again, not because I wanted him to return the gesture, but because I didn't want him to. I wanted to blame someone else, wanted to deflect my sadness towards this stranger. Naturally, he smiled back, and I saw he had a good set of teeth. White. He'd looked after them well.

As I placed my foot on the landing next to him, he put a hand on my shoulder. A fatherly touch.

"No need to be sad," the man who could be Teddy said. "This is the start and the end of it."

Or at least that's what I thought he said, but maybe some of the words got swallowed up by his beard. Before I had time to raise a question, he was already a quarter of the way down the stairs, and his body language told me he had no intention of stopping.

Confused and sad, I made my way along the corridor to the flat. I didn't want to go in, didn't want to go through to our empty home beyond. It felt like if I did that, I would never see Freya again, but what else could I do? There was nowhere else to go. No one else to talk to.

I found the key on my fob, placed its crooked teeth into the lock, and twisted. I sighed, looked down and pushed the door open as I had done thousands of times before.

*

I was back in Songström, back in the hut when I should have been in my flat. My foot clunked on wooden floorboards, and in front of me was the open plan living area. I could hardly breathe.

"Come in," said a female voice.

I could see a window in the facing wall; it showed a vista bathed in daylight. This was another time as well as another place. I looked around for the owner of the voice, but no one was there. I looked behind me. Through the door I could see the hallway of my flats. I could retreat, I could run away from this madness, but what good would running do? I'd just continue to worry about Songström, and I'd done enough of that.

"Please come in," the voice repeated. It was not the voice of the maggot woman I'd encountered in my youth. "Do you know where you are?"

"I'm in Songström," I replied.

"Songström," she agreed. "I'm sorry to bring you here, but this place has power, and it is power I can use right now."

"I didn't think this place existed. I thought I'd dreamt it."

"Liar. You just didn't want to face what it meant if it did exist, and that's okay. Who's going to believe you?"

I stayed near the door.

"Please, come in. It doesn't matter whether you're one foot inside or twenty. You are here."

"The old woman..." I started.

"Isn't here. Can't be here. You are safe. Freya, however, needs your help."

"Where is she?"

"Looking for you."

A numbness crept over the nape of my neck, and slowly descended towards my chest.

"Looking for me?" I croaked.

"She is. She needs the Sikkilite, Sammel."

"But she has it," I said. "It's tied around her neck."

"Maybe once, but not anymore," the woman said. "She needs you to get it to her. Needs you to find her so she can have it, do you understand?"

"Not really."

"You have to do what I say. You haven't many friends, Sammel Ahlberg. Will you do what I say? Will you find Freya?"

"Okay." I nodded. "Where's the Sikkilite?"

"In your pocket."

I touched my trouser pocket. She was right. The Sikkilite was there.

"How did I get it?"

"You've always had it."

I thought about that. Thought about tying it around Freya's neck earlier that day. I could see it, I was sure, but the more I tried to picture it, the harder it became to remember.

"Who are you?"

"I am many people. A ghost, perhaps. Or part of a ghost. It's hard to tell. But I am not in need of saving, Sammel. You need to find Freya."

"Do you know where she is?"

"If I did, I would have told you. I can only reach out to you because you have the Sikkilite; beyond this my sight is limited. You must find her, and soon. For your own sake, it must be soon."

She sounded certain. This was the path I had to take, and I could not deviate.

"Should I call the police?"

"No," she said. "Songström has friends there. You must find her without their help."

"I don't know where I should start." A darkness flashed over the hut. "What was that?"

"You must go. I thought you were safe, but they're returning. Leave now, Sammel, and find her."

Another wave of darkness, slightly longer this time, and I had the impression of a dark shape swooping down out of the sky, blocking out the sun in ever decreasing circles.

I turned and left as quickly as possible. It didn't matter that I was many times older than when I'd first visited Songström, I was still just as scared.

*

I didn't stay in the flat. I went down the stairs, out of the door and across the road to the park opposite. It was dark there. I checked my phone, nine forty PM; no messages.

Freya could be anywhere. That was the fact I had to accept. I stood and stared at the blackness and tried to think of my next move. Sometimes I find it difficult to think. Sometimes my head is so full of thoughts even the simplest of situations is confusing.

My pack was heavy. Heavier than usual. I tried to think why and realised I still had Freya's bag in it. I smiled. Her bag must hold a clue, that must be why the woman in the bathroom had let it be found. I swung the pack off my shoulder, undid the fasteners and saw the straps of her handbag poking out of the top.

I paused. I didn't want to go through it. These were Freya's private things, and it made me feel nervous. Her bag should be sacred, was sacred, but what else could I do? However hard I tried to think of another way of finding her, this search was the only answer I could come up with.

I sat on a bench under one of the few park lights and inventoried her belongings.

- Magazine – it wasn't one of those celebrity ones. This one was about cooking. Oddly, I couldn't remember her ever cooking. That's why we met at the café.

- Sanitary towels – I tried to be discreet about these, not looking too much, but I did note they were ones we sold at the supermarket. They were on special offer at the moment, too.

- Phone charger – one that fits any phone. It fitted my phone. I didn't know how long she'd had it.

- Purse – a small brown purse with some coins in. No notes. She didn't carry around a lot of money. You didn't need to, nowadays.

- Two books – one fiction, one factual – both with bookmarks. Freya liked books. She was better at reading than me. I found it hard to concentrate for long periods of time.

- Contact lens solution – the supermarket sold this, too. I guessed the supermarket sold a lot of things.

- Glasses case, with glasses in – Freya's glasses were simple. She didn't want anything too frilly. She used them when she was looking at the prices of things.

- Hand sanitiser – we shared a need to have clean hands. It was important. This hand sanitiser looked new.

- Moisturiser – up until recently, I didn't really know what moisturiser was. This one Freya used on her hands. I'd tried some of it, too, but didn't see any difference. Apart from the smell.

- Sunglasses – As non-frilly as the glasses. One arm was slightly skewed and there was a scuff-mark on one of the lenses like they might have been stepped on.

- Pens – assorted. Some working, some not.

- Mints – mostly eaten.

- Lip balm – scuffed and nearly empty.

- Tissues – clean.

- A set of keys – for the flat most likely.

Nothing useful. Nothing that told me where she might be. I looked at the dark interior again, ran my fingers around the cloth inside. There were two zipped pockets I'd missed. The first was full of receipts, too many to look at. The second, on the opposite side, held more receipts, a bank card, and another keyring. On the keyring were two keys and one half of a metal heart.

I'd never seen the bank card or the keys. I looked at the receipts stored with it. Grocery receipts, coffee shop receipts, and one bar receipt, folded down small. The date on it was the middle of last month. The amount could have been a single expensive drink or two cheaper ones.

I don't drink, and find the idea of bars intimidating. My mother drank, and no one spoke about it. No one needed to. She drank and I didn't like it. She drank and she said things, and I didn't like the things she said.

I knew the receipt wasn't much, but it was something. The bar was in town, along the seafront. Too far to walk, but only a fifteen-minute cycle ride. I went back to the flats, retrieved my bike, and left.

*

Sometimes I don't understand what happens. I wake up, or come to, and I'm not where I'm supposed to be, not doing the things I was supposed to be doing.

The front wheel of my bicycle hit a small kerb and I started to tumble to the left. Part of me, the part I'm not in control of, reacted before I had fully taken in the situation, twisting my body so I landed safely on my side.

It took me a moment to get my bearings. I was at the old shopping centre.

There are places I avoid, no matter the time of day, no matter if it's crowded or empty. The old shopping centre was one of them. There'd been a time when it was lined with shops, full of hope, but, one by one, over the years, they had closed, leaving nothing but a tunnel where the echoes followed you home. It was a sad place, but that wasn't why I avoided it.

Now, at night, the shadows were long and mocking, creeping and reaching beyond their natural limitations, wanting a piece of me. I pushed myself up into a sitting position, and looked around. The bicycle was okay, the front wheel still spinning, emitting the slow clicking of misused machinery.

Then, under the clicking, came another noise. Somewhere in front of me, something was being knocked or kicked.

"Leave me alone," I said.

A whistle then. A far-off whistle, not of a person, but of something my brain didn't want to recognise.

Out of the darkness came a man carrying a tray, smiling a smile not even his mother could have loved. I scrambled to my feet.

"A customer," he said, grinning, looking me up and down.

Behind him a woman appeared, wearing a bloodied apron over clothes from another age.

"Are you hungry today?" she asked.

"No," I told her. "Leave me alone."

"Oh, bless," the woman said. "He thought I was talking to him."

Another person, a young boy in a cap emerged from the gloom.

"There's not much to him," the boy said.

"There's fear," the woman replied, licking her lips. "I like fear."

"But what about the joy?" the boy whined. "I'm hungry. I've been hungry for ages."

"I have joy," I said. "Don't tell me I don't have joy." Sometimes I say things and I don't know why I'm saying them.

The man spoke next. "The boy's right. There's no joy there. But there's loss, can you feel it? So much loss, I wouldn't have to eat for a year."

I shook my head. "I have no loss," my mouth said. "I might not have my parents, but I have no loss."

All three laughed then, and they were much closer than I thought. They laughed and I felt giddy. I felt like I was going to be sick.

The whistle came again, and this time I knew what it was. A train, though not the hoot of a modern-day engine. This was the whistle of a steam train, and I instantly knew these people had been sent from Songström.

"Don't you know where you are?" the woman said.

I looked around. All of us were now standing on railway tracks.

"Why am I here?" I asked, but they didn't reply. They simply looked at me, hunger in their eyes.

Then there was a light. It wasn't very bright, but it was there, and it was getting bigger. The train was approaching.

"What are we waiting for?" the boy asked. "Why do we always have to wait?"

The woman cocked her head and smiled. "Won't be long, boy," she said.

"No, won't be long," said the man.

The train kept on coming, and I wanted to run. They were blocking my exit either side, so all I could do was set off, down the tracks, away from the train. They laughed even harder then. I didn't blame them. It must have looked stupid. I was never going to outrun a train, steam-powered or otherwise.

Still, I ran, and when their laughing grew no quieter, I knew they were right there with me, waiting. I was going to be hit, my body was going to be splintered, and they were waiting for it, waiting till they could have their fill. All apart from the boy, who wanted joy.

I tripped and fell, and that was that. I waited to be hit. Waited as the whistle blew, as the noise became deafening. I was scared, so scared. My life didn't flash before me as I'd heard. Only one thing entered my mind. One image. One word.

"Sikkilite," I whispered.

I opened my eyes and I was on the ground at the shopping centre. I saw double, and my head hurt. About a foot ahead of me the front wheel of my bicycle was still turning.

*

It was ten minutes before I felt well enough to get back on the bike and keep moving. This time I concentrated on what I was doing.

I couldn't shake what the boy had said, about having no joy. That made me angry, and being angry kept me alert. I tried to think of a joyous moment in my life. I'd had them, I knew that, but I couldn't remember exactly when. This, in turn, made me even angrier. I'd had a happy childhood. My father had seen to it.

"Watch it!" someone shouted from nearby. I snapped back and immediately applied my brakes, managing to stop the bicycle just before I collided with an open car door.

The man stood motionless behind the door, almost daring me to hit it. For a moment, I was worried he might be a demon sent from Songström, but then nothing strange happened. I smiled at him.

"Sorry," I lied. He made a noise like "hmph", got into his car and closed the door. I cycled past him.

*

I locked the bike somewhere I hoped was safe and walked along the edge of the pavement closest to the buildings. People were walking around. Some couples, some groups, some individuals. I felt my heart beating faster and tried to breathe slowly like I'd taught myself to do.

"They're just like me," I said to myself. Of course, they were, but Songström was a place and yet not a place, so I shouldn't have been so relaxed. I needed to be on my guard.

"Got a ciggy?" a man said beside me as I walked past a narrow alley. I flinched from the sound. "It's all right, I'm not going to hurt you." I kept walking, not saying anything. A few paces further on, he said "arse," and that was that.

Breathe.

*

Most of the bars were in one area. I supposed it made sense when you thought how difficult it was for drunk people to walk very far. I passed by darkened cafes, shuttered clothes shops, and empty convenience stores, and felt happier for being near them. I often imagined parts of me being closed, little metal grilles pulled down over my memories, my experiences. I didn't know how many memories were locked away. Maybe hundreds, maybe many more. What I did know was everything felt better for them being there.

I was closer now. The bar I wanted was along the seafront, opposite the deep, dead water. I could already hear the waves. Sometimes I woke from dreams, and the dreams were of me standing in the sea up to my waist, looking out to the horizon, with no understanding of what I might be searching for. I'd feel the cold water lapping at my legs, my crotch, my midriff. I wouldn't know whether the tide was coming in or going out. It might be doing neither. It might just be holding me there.

These were strange, recurring dreams. I didn't think anything of them. They were not portents nor warnings. They were neither memories nor worries. It was just me and the sea, and... someone else. I knew there was someone else there in the dreams. I couldn't hear them or see them, but they stood behind me, silently, their arms outstretched, reaching, their fingertips only ever an inch or so away from my back. I supposed if I tried hard enough I could have turned around, but I never did, and that made me wonder, did I want them to reach me? Was the reaching the thing that made me feel better? Would turning around ruin the enjoyment of the dream?

I crossed the road and stood on the promenade, opposite the bar where the receipt was from, looking at the people inside. They looked like they were enjoying themselves and I smiled. I might never understand these interactions, but it didn't matter. I didn't understand how trees grew, or bees collected honey. Understanding something was revealing the trick, knowing how it worked, and, most of the time, I preferred to remain in awe of the magic.

*

Freya was still magic. She was a whole box of tricks. A whole magic circle full of tricks. She was incomprehensible, a mermaid in the modern world. A superhero in a world of mortals. Freya was a billion stars so far off you only saw a billionth of their brightness, yet still it made you wonder.

She held my hand. Until that moment, my hand had only ever been a tool, an implement for the everyday. But when Freya placed her hand within, it suddenly became a light to all the experiences, which had long been hidden behind the darkness.

*

The promenade stretched off and curved like it went on forever, and in a way, it did. If I was to walk one way or the other for long enough, I would eventually arrive back at this same spot. Everything is finite. The truth of this made me lose my balance momentarily.

There was no sanctuary to be had here. The lights shone down, shone out, and I was bathed in an orange, sickly glow.

Where was Freya? Why did she have a receipt from a bar?

I didn't know. I couldn't know. But soon I might know. It felt like that thing was reaching for my back, and this evening I was going to turn around and look, look it straight in the eye, though most likely it was a monster.

There was the noise of the sea on one side, and noises from the bar on the other. I liked neither, but the sea would wait, would skulk in my dreams. The bar was more immediate. Meetings are transitory, and sometimes good things happen, and sometimes bad. Freya had been at this bar, and I needed to find out why.

I set off towards it, passing tropical trees, bent in the wind as if in prayer to some far-off, near-forgotten god.

I crossed the road and took out my wallet. I didn't know if I'd have enough money. I needed money if I was to enter a bar. As it turned out, I had plenty, more than I'd ever need for anything on offer inside. I walked up the steps, and looked at the sign above the door. It might have been the angle I was standing at, or perhaps my tiredness, but I couldn't understand what the sign read. All I could tell, was that it occupied at least two floors of the building.

Three people came out and I let them pass. I didn't look at them too closely, but they seemed to be happy.

*

A man walks into a bar. That was the beginning to a joke I'd read on the internet. I couldn't remember the punchline, any of the punchlines; my brain doesn't possess the ability to remember them. Now, I was that man, and it struck me that, when the man was me, it didn't need a punchline. I was the punchline.

There were people everywhere. All of them holding drinks, some of them holding two. A lot of the men held bottles. I guessed they were beer. A lot of the women held bottles too. There was so much noise and so many colours.

I could smell the alcohol instantly. It was chemical and cloying. I put my head down, tried my best to breathe only through my mouth, but found that worse. I didn't want to faint. Not in here; not in front of all these people.

I imagined myself somewhere else. On a warm beach, waiting to be served with cool drinks. Sometimes when I think of other places, I wonder if they exist. I wonder if there is another version of me actually there, acting out my thoughts. And then I wonder if they're the ones thinking about me, and if I'm the one acting out their thoughts. I think that should make me worry, but in fact it makes me calm, because if all I'm doing is acting out someone else's thoughts, then I can't be responsible for anything I do.

I thought of this man on the beach, and he thought about me, and I gripped my money a little tighter, turned right into the larger room, and headed towards the bar.

It took me a while to get served. I ordered a drink, paid for it, and held it in my hand like it was for someone else. It was busy. I waited, watching as the staff did their routines. Serving, smiling, collecting. There was a pattern there. I liked the pattern. I expected no one else could see it, no one else was looking for it. Serve, smile, collect.

I drank my drink slowly. It wasn't alcoholic. It was a lemonade and lime. It was refreshing. As I drank, I continued to watch the people in the bar, particularly noting the waitress responsible for bringing back the empty glasses and bottles. I thought they might be my best chance of asking about Freya.

I watched and waited. She patrolled every ten minutes. The bar died down ever so slightly, and when she started her collection once more, I went over to the window at the front of the room and waited.

She came past a minute later. It was her routine.

"Hello," I said to her.

"What?"

"Hello," I repeated.

"Can I get you something?" She was short, her hair shaved on one side of her head. The hair she did have had subtle streaks of purple and blue, and fell just below her shoulder, like she was due a haircut. She had a young face.

"I'd like to ask you a question," I said to her. She looked at me warily.

"Are you a weirdo?"

I thought about this question. "I find it hard to speak to people," I told her. "I'm sorry."

She seemed to soften a bit at this admission. "No need to apologise," she said. "I'm a bit of a loner, too. How can I help?"

"I'm looking for my friend. I wondered whether you might have seen her."

She looked at me, and then at the bottles in her hands.

"Look, I've got to get these back to the bar. Follow me and we can keep talking."

She moved through the people very skilfully, weaving deftly between each of them. She didn't touch anyone, not even once. At the bar, she placed the bottles and glasses on the counter and turned back to me.

"Have you got a picture of her?"

"I think so," I said. I retrieved my wallet and flicked through it. Something must have happened to my picture of her. I must have dropped it. I looked at the waitress. "I'm sorry, I don't think I have."

Her face made an expression, which said she felt sorry for me. That was okay.

"Right, well then, not sure how I can help. What's her name?"

"Freya," I said.

"Surname?"

"My surname is Ahlberg," I said.

"What about hers? Do you know what her surname is?"

I left then. I couldn't remember her surname. Freya's surname. It was a blank, so I left. I heard the barmaid call out a couple of times as I went. I didn't hear what she said, just the pitch of her voice.

*

I went over to the promenade and found a shelter to sit in. I still had my drink in my hand. Perhaps that was what she'd been shouting about. The shelter was quite clean. The paint had recently been applied. I felt safe.

I closed my eyes.

I was dreaming. I knew it. I knew it in the way I knew everything. The sky was still dark, the waves were still breaking on the shoreline, but I wasn't awake.

Someone walked by, then a couple, then three people. None of them looked at me, and they spoke in a language all of their own. I was not allowed in. I was an outsider. I sat up. In my hand was the drink I had bought at the bar, but it was no longer a shade of green. Now it was red. On the beach I heard the sound of pebbles, but there were no pebbles when I looked, and beyond it the sea was still.

To the left was the pier, and something was under it. Something dark was under the pier. I wanted to stay away and yet now I was standing, and now I was walking, and now my feet were walking on the pebbles that were not there.

"Stop," I said, I wanted to say, but nothing came out.

The man with the beard in my block of flats, Teddy, walked past, and he said, "It's started now." Then he was gone and he was never there, and still my feet took one step in front of the other and I was walking to meet with the thing that hid in the darkness under the pier.

It wanted me. It was the thing in Songström, the thing in the air, and it raged. It boiled. It shook. It was all consuming, and it was something I shouldn't be allowing to control me.

"Stop," I said, and this time the words were spoken.

I turned back towards the promenade, and the people who'd walked by were now looking out at me, watching me and eating ice-cream in cones like mechanical tourists. I wanted to shout at them to go away, but they would never go away. They were the onlookers. The parts of people that have to be satiated with the misfortune of others.

I hated them. I understood them.

The thing under the pier said, "Keep walking," and I did. Only a few steps. And as I walked I saw onlookers on the pier, too, leaning over precariously, all just a slip away from falling to the sand.

"Keep walking," it said, and, somehow, I knew it wasn't talking to me. I stopped, and as I did, a figure pushed past, a man I recognised.

"Bobby," I called out, but he didn't stop or turn. "Bobby," I said again. I could have shouted it, but shouting wouldn't have worked. "Bobby," I said for a third time, and this time he held up his arm, and showed me the okay sign. "Don't go," I said. "You won't survive."

Then I saw Bobby shrug, yet he didn't stop. I walked as quickly as I dared, but he grew no closer and got no further away.

Then Bobby was gone, and in his place on the sand, the Sikkilite sat, and the thing under the pier started to emerge. One after another, single strands of darkness crept from under the boards. It was dislodging itself, and the pier shook with strain.

"Stay there," I called out.

"You haven't found her," it replied. "I don't need you. And if I don't need you…"

"No, not yet. I'll find her. I will."

"You've taken too long."

I frowned. "I've only been looking this evening."

It paused then. The creaking stopped and I could feel it thinking.

"Just one evening," it said. It could have been mocking me. It could have been agreeing. "Very well, then. I will allow you six more days. No more. Then I'll come and get you, and you will be lost."

"Why me?" I asked.

The blackness shouted then.

"I want everything!" it bellowed. "I get everything. You are part of everything, Sammel, whether you know it or not."

"I know who I am," I spat, angrily. "And I know what you are. Leave me alone. Leave everyone alone." I flinched at the sound of my voice. It didn't sound like me.

"Six days," the darkness repeated, sinking back beneath the pier. "Six days."

The onlookers turned and walked away, and I was alone on the beach with the Sikkilite in front of me.

*

I opened my eyes, and I was back on the bench, sitting down and looking out to sea. I patted my pocket, and felt the Sikkilite there.

"You left this," said a woman's voice. I turned and saw the collector of glasses. She held out an envelope with something inside.

"Where did I leave it? I don't remember having an envelope."

"Not this evening. I thought I recognised you, and then I remembered the envelope. I brought it back to you."

I reached up and took the envelope. "When did I leave it?"

"A couple of weeks ago, I think. Yes. That's right. You were in here. Drinking the same drink. On your own."

"Thank you," I said. The girl smiled and went back towards the bar.

*

I didn't want to open the envelope, but I had little choice. The darkness had given me six days to find Freya. It wanted me to fail. It wanted to come and take me. To consume me.

Inside the envelope were dozens of photographs. Printed out on square paper which reminded me of an instant camera. I closed my eyes and counted each square. If I'd looked at them, I might forget to count them, and then I wouldn't know how many there had been to begin with.

Thirty. There were thirty photos. I looked at one of them. It was of me, walking down the road. Nothing special. It was daytime, and I was walking past some shops. A very strange subject for a photograph. Another one was of me, as well. This time I was locking my bicycle to a lamppost near the station. There was no one else in the photograph. Just me.

I was the subject of the next one. And the next one. I spread the rest of them out as best I could. They were all of me. Why? And why didn't I remember leaving them in the bar? And why had I been in the bar?

I thought about what I should do next. My breathing was becoming haphazard, and I was starting to lose my concentration. Thirty photographs. It was too much information. Too much unorganised data. I needed to organise it. Needed to bring it into something I could understand.

I found a pencil and one of my smaller notebooks in my bag. I wasn't sure if the order they'd been placed inside the envelope had been important, but I'd been careful not to mix them up when I'd spread them out. Carefully, I picked each one up and stacked them on the bench to the left of me.

I found the next clear page in the notebook and wrote the numbers one to fifteen down the first page, turned it up and over, and wrote sixteen to thirty down the next. There were exactly fifteen lines per page. I began to feel better.

These were the photographs, as they were in the envelope.

1.   Sammel pulling the curtains of his flat window.
2.   Sammel eating toast looking out of the window.
3.   Sammel walking out of the flat.

4.   Sammel stopped on his bike waiting at some traffic lights.

5.   Sammel locking his bicycle to a lamppost.

6.   Sammel walking down the street.

7.   Sammel speaking to the man who sits near the newsagents, who doesn't have a home.

8.   Sammel walking to the newsagents.

9.   Sammel leaving the newsagents reading a magazine.

10.   Sammel sitting on a bench in the park.

11.   Sammel feeding the birds.

12.   Sammel checking his watch for the time on a street corner.

13.   Sammel entering the supermarket door to start work.

14.   Sammel standing by the vegetables display, organising them by date and size. You cannot tell this from the picture, I just happen to know that's what I do.

15.   Sammel looking out of the window of the shop during a short break.

16.   Sammel in the café at lunchtime eating dinner.

17.   Sammel looking off, away from camera at something.

18.   Sammel leaving the café and going back to work.

19.   Sammel standing near the tills.

20.   Sammel talking to the supermarket manager.

21. Sammel leaving work.

22. Sammel sitting in the café, drinking a cup of tea.

23. Sammel looking at his telephone.

24. Sammel with his telephone to his ear.

25. Sammel talking to the man without a home again.

26. Sammel walking back to his bicycle.

27. Sammel riding off on his bicycle.

28. Sammel arriving back at the flat.

29. Sammel at the window of the flat looking out.

30. Sammel closing the curtains.

It was easy to see what these were. Someone had documented my day. Someone had followed me for the whole day taking pictures and I hadn't noticed them. It was strange. I suddenly had the thought they might be watching me now, taking more photographs to put in an envelope. I looked up and around, slowly and carefully concentrating on each person I could see. They all seemed focused on their own conversations. I supposed there was no need to take any more pictures. This was how I lived my life. Thirty pictures from when I woke up, to when I fell asleep. They applied to any day. Any normal day. Was today normal? No. Today, Freya was missing.

Was the number thirty important? It seemed very specific. Much more specific than thirty-one or twenty-six. I didn't know what the significance was. Perhaps I would work it out later.

Another thing was bothering me. The magazine. Without the magazine, this could have been any day in the past couple of years. But I knew the cover of the magazine. I used to buy more than one per week, but realised I had to cut down. I decided only buying one was both acceptable and affordable.

The magazine I'd been reading in the photographs had come out last month. I'd picked it up on the Wednesday morning like always. I thought about this. I thought about it over the noise of the waves. I thought about it as people moved past me along the promenade.

I looked through the pictures again. I didn't need to. I'd already catalogued them, but I did it anyway. I brought them up to my eye, tried to see if the photographer had been careless with the reflections. There was nothing. Whoever had taken the pictures had been very careful. Or very lucky.

A thought struck me, and I riffled through the thirty images until I found the one of me entering the supermarket. I looked at the pole to the side of the door. I looked at the camera on top of the pole, and I looked at the way it had been facing.

That's it. That's what I could do next. The camera had been pointing at the photographer. The tapes are held for a month before being erased. I looked at my watch. It was ten thirty-four PM. The supermarket was open till eleven on Fridays. The boss would have gone home. There would be a skeleton crew on now. I could go and speak to Garrick. He would be on security.

I put the photographs back into the envelope, closed the flap and put it in my pocket. There wasn't a lot of time till the supermarket closed. I stood up and stepped out of the shelter. I had to get my bicycle, and I had to go to the supermarket.

*

When I work at the supermarket, I leave my bicycle in a part of town that's busy. I've always figured if it's busy, it's less likely people will steal it. It also means I have a ten-minute walk through a park from where I chain it up, and that way I fit in twenty minutes of walking each day, which, like the cycling, is good for me. I try and do a lot of exercise. It keeps me fit, but most of all, it keeps me busy.

A lot of the time I cycle on the pavements, because it makes me feel safer. Since this was the second trip to the supermarket today, I was happy to forgo the walk, and ride through the park instead. The park isn't massive, but it's nice, and only takes a few minutes to negotiate from one side to the other. There is a building in the middle of the park. A place that serves tea and coffee.

*

I've always felt watched. Always. Sometimes the feeling's stronger, and sometimes it's hardly there at all. As I cycled through the park, things peered at me from the trees, *were* the trees. They peered at me from the dark spaces, from between their leaves and branches.

"You can't get me," I said, as bravely as possible. It didn't matter. They didn't want me today. Today they were content with watching,

56

with knowing where I was. They had a plan in mind, I could tell. The watchers always had a plan.

After the park, I rode along the pavement to the shops. Because I was in a particular rush, I actually brought my bicycle inside the supermarket, which gained the attention of a couple of late-night shoppers. I walked the bike through the plastic slats and into the small warehouse at the back. This was where security had an office barely big enough to fit two people.

I didn't bother to lock my bicycle, leaning it up, instead, against the tall metal racks that held the large boxes of cereals. I knocked on the security door, waking Garrick up. He peered at me, and I realised I still had my cycle helmet on.

I raised two thumbs in my normal gesture of hello, and it seemed to do the trick. He got up slowly, removing his feet, one by one, from under the desk, before shuffling to the door and twisting the handle on the other side. The door opened a crack.

"What do you want, Sammel?" he asked.

"I wondered whether I could look at one of the security tapes from two Wednesdays ago. From the start of my shift, to be precise."

"I can't do that. It's against company policy."

"What policy?" I asked him.

"You don't work here anymore."

Garrick had taken to saying that lately. I assumed it was some sort of humourless joke.

"I do work here, Garrick," I told him. "Besides, what if I told you someone is planning to rob the store, and I think they were caught on camera on that Wednesday?"

That seemed to wake him up a bit. "Rob the store? When?"

"I don't know. I was hoping to work it out after seeing the footage."

Garrick thought for a moment. "Tell you what," he said, suppressing a yawn. "Why don't you tell me exactly when you arrived and I'll take a look at it now?"

"No. it needs to be me who looks at it."

"It's against company policy."

"If you don't let me look at it, I'll tell them you ignored me, and if we get robbed, you'll be sacked."

Garrick narrowed his eyes. "You know, you really are a little prick, Sammel."

"Sometimes I find it difficult to get on with people," I replied.

"No, you're just a prick."

Garrick stepped back and opened the door marginally wider for me to enter.

"Thank you," I said.

"Fuck you," he said.

He sat back in the far chair, and opened a drawer beside him. In the drawer were a series of tapes. I sat down next to him.

"Which camera?" he asked without looking up.

"The one facing away from the door."

"And what time?"

"The morning one."

Garrick shot me a look. He was annoyed. He'd wanted me to tell him exactly when, tried to catch me off-guard, but I hadn't fallen for it. He picked out a tape, loaded it into the second machine, and pressed a button.

He put his hand on a dial on the front of the machine and moved it clockwise. An image appeared on the screen and spun forwards.

"When?"

"Can I have a go, please? It'll be quicker if I do it."

"Who the hell employed you in the first place?" he asked, rhetorically. "I bet it was that idiot, Ben. Was it?"

I didn't answer. It was indeed Ben who had interviewed me, and he'd been kind enough to give me a chance. He'd told me I reminded him of a boy he'd known at school whom he hadn't been nice to. He said employing me was a chance to redeem himself. I wanted to tell him that was a stupid thought. Helping me would not help that boy, that's not how anything worked.

When Garrick saw I wasn't going to answer him, he let go of the knob and pushed his chair back.

"Fill your fucking boots."

Carefully, I turned the knob forwards by tiny little increments, until minutes were zipping by on screen. I wasn't sure how Garrick didn't know what time I arrived at the store. I only do one type of day shift, and I always arrived at eight fifty-six. I guess it just highlighted how unobservant he was. Perhaps Ben had interviewed him, too. Perhaps Garrick reminded Ben of the same boy. Maybe there was no boy. Perhaps Ben was just lazy and employed the first person who applied for the job.

The clock in the corner of the screen sped through the six AM hour. It was surprising how many people were out at that time in the morning. On to seven AM; more people walking past the camera at amusingly high speeds. Finally, it reached eight AM. There were lots of people now, drinking coffee from takeaway cups.

"Are you sure you want to do this?" Garrick said from my left. It was a strange question, but not one I thought much about. It was an annoying buzz in my ear, nothing else. I continued to watch, slowing the speed till we were at eight fifty-three. I assumed the photographer might have had to appear slightly earlier in order to prepare for my arrival.

At eight fifty-four they arrived. They wore a light-coloured hooded top, tight jeans that hugged their thin legs and white trainers. Their frame looked thin; gaunt was the word that struck me.

"There they are," I told Garrick.

I heard Garrick sigh beside me. "I'm sorry," he said.

"It's not your..." I began, then felt a pain in my side. I looked down. Garrick had his hand around a small knife, which was pressed into my midriff. "What are you doing?" I said, grabbing his hand, stopping it doing any more damage.

"They told me I had to," he replied. "They told me I had to."

I held his hand as firmly as I could. It was at an odd angle, so wasn't as easy as it should have been. Fortunately, he wasn't trying very hard, and as I increased the pressure, the knife came out.

"They said I had to kill you. I didn't want to. I don't like you, but I didn't want to kill you."

I stood up slowly, feeling blood on my fingers. "Who told you? Who said you had to kill me?"

Garrick pointed to the image on the screen. "They threatened me. Threatened my mother. They said they'd kill her if you found out. Now you've found out."

"Why do they want to kill me?" I asked. "Have I done something?" I couldn't take it in. I was trying my best to work out everything that had just happened.

"Self-defence," Garrick said. "They said to say it was self-defence. They didn't tell me why."

"Where are the keys?"

"Keys?"

"To the shop. I need the back door key. I need to slip out that way. If they're watching the shop, they'll have seen me come in, and they'll be waiting to see if I leave. You stay here, do you understand? I'll go to your mother's, and bring her here. I'll make this right."

Garrick looked at me for a moment, unsure. Then he handed me a set of keys. "Here," he said. I took them and went to the door. "I haven't told you where she lives."

"You live with her?" I asked. Garrick nodded. "Then I know where she lives. Cover the glass in the door. They must think I'm dead."

Garrick opened a drawer near him. Inside was a supply of bandages and gauze pads. "Take these," he said. "Apply pressure."

I nodded, opened the door and checked the path to the back of the shop. It looked clear. "Stay in here," I said to Garrick. He half-nodded. He looked sick.

*

I knew which was the key for the backdoor. That's the sort of detail I keep an eye out for. If things aren't going too well with me, I let my brain get involved with everything nearby, let it become part of other people's lives. That's how I knew where Garrick lived. Not just Garrick. I knew where everyone who worked at the store lived. It sounded weird, but it was just something I did to keep going. I don't follow them. I just picked up details from things they said, or the direction they'd enter work from. Or sometimes, if I couldn't work it out, the internet.

I understood the internet. The way pages were structured, or, moreover, the way they weren't. The way you could be looking for one thing, and without realising, end up reading a page on something else entirely. That was often how my brain worked.

Garrick lived three roads away, above a carpet shop. It was a two bedroom flat, and he'd lived there for more years than I could search online for. I grabbed my bicycle, exited the store, and rode slowly, not wanting to exert myself, still not knowing exactly how bad my stab wound was.

I found it difficult to comprehend what had just happened. Someone had threatened Garrick, threatened his mother, and told him to kill me. It made no sense.

Had they somehow predicted I'd go to the supermarket after seeing the photographs? Had they planned that? Or was it just a precaution? And if it was a precaution, how many other people had they threatened? How many other people had been told to kill me if I came snooping?

The traffic was surprisingly heavy considering the lateness of the hour. I rode on the pavement as much as I could, holding my side with one hand, gripping the handlebars firmly with the other. A lot of people must have seen the blood on my shirt, or on my hand, and I was expecting to be stopped with every corner I turned, yet I reached the small parade of shops where Garrick lived, without incident.

I stopped outside for a moment to catch my breath, then rode around to the back to where the stairs led up to the flats, and tucked my bike out of sight behind some large pieces of cardboard put out for recycling.

It was quiet behind the shops; the sort of place where people rarely spoke to one another, and only thieves spent any real time getting to know. It wasn't a welcoming place.

My breathing became laboured as I climbed the steps, and when I reached the landing, which ran along the back of the flats, I paused for a couple of moments. I didn't know what I was about to walk in on. Part of me wanted to go back, I could feel it pushing my feet to go back down the steps, to return to my own flat, and sleep for a long time.

"No," I said, quietly.

I moved along the passageway, Garrick's key in my hand, but when I reached his flat, the door was already ajar.

"Mrs Garrick?" I called out softly. "Are you there?"

I pushed the front door open, and waited. The hallway beyond was dark, but I could reach the light switch from outside. I flicked it, not expecting it to work. It did.

There was something about the hallway's tidiness that surprised me. A thin table lay against the wall, and on it was a small vase of fake flowers, and a brass dish for letters. There was a picture on the wall, a bright landscape of somewhere idyllic in summer.

I stepped into the hallway, and glanced beyond the first open door. It was a bedroom. His mother's if I had to guess. There were a lot of flowers everywhere. On the wallpaper, on the bedspread.

"Mrs Garrick," I called again. I wasn't expecting an answer. The flat seemed deserted. "Your son sent me. I'm here to make sure you're okay."

The bathroom and kitchen were clear, as was the second bedroom, and I began to panic. I was running out of places she could be. If she wasn't here...

I saw her as soon as I entered the lounge, asleep in a chair, head forward, resting on her chest. The light was off, and I didn't want to wake her by turning it on.

"Mrs Garrick?" I said softly. I took a step closer. "Can you hear me?" A step closer. "Your son sent me."

I was almost in front of her, now, the only light in the room coming from the muted television, showing some old black and white Western. I glanced at it, but I didn't recognise the film.

I put my hand on Garrick's mother's shoulder, and crouched by her legs to seem less intimidating.

"Mrs. Garrick?" I said, looking up into her face.

I fell backwards, away from her, trying to understand, trying not to flee. Mrs Garrick's face was gone. In its place was a hole, almost perfectly oval, where her face should have been. Not just her face, but the whole front of her skull. It was gone, scooped out.

My back hit the television and I couldn't go any further. I didn't want to look at her. I wanted to look at the television, wanted to pretend I hadn't just seen what I'd seen.

I knew who'd done it. The old woman in Songström. It was what she'd promised to do to me; to eat my face. She had been here, in Garrick's flat, and her mother hadn't been strong enough to break free. Rage swelled within me. How dare she do this to an innocent person?

It had been Songström that had taken the pictures. It was watching me. As Teddy had warned me, something had started and now Songström didn't want it to continue. They had told Garrick to kill me if I came looking.

Why Mrs Garrick though? Was Songström clever enough to know I'd come here? Did it know every thought I'd have before I'd thought it? Was it ahead of me, or was I behind?

I looked at her for a moment, at the back of her skull that was now visible. It was strange. Without her features, it was difficult to picture her as a person. On a table beside the chair sat a photo of her and Garrick, taken at least twenty years ago. They looked, not happy, but serene. They had posed for the camera.

I heard sirens then, and wasn't sure how long they'd been going for. They sounded a little way off, and the only thing I could do was to get out while I could. I had to warn Garrick. I had to give him this terrible, awful, news.

I didn't make it back to the supermarket. By the time I'd found and retrieved the bicycle, I was feeling faint and slightly nauseous. Blood continued to ooze from my side, and I realised I'd need medical attention before I could make any meaningful progress. I pointed the bicycle in the direction of the hospital and set off.

I had to be careful what I told the doctors. I'd have to give them a story that wouldn't arouse suspicion. If my excuse wasn't good enough, they might think I'd harmed myself. If I told them it was a mugging, they might get the police involved, and I couldn't trust the police. I'd have to say it was an accident; that I'd fallen off my bike, and landed on something sharp.

It was a poor excuse, I knew, but I had little choice.

I rode slowly to the hospital A & E, abandoned the bicycle near the front entrance and stood in line for the reception desk. As events turned out, I needn't have worried about what I'd tell them. I collapsed before I'd reached the window.

When I came to, my wound had been stitched, and I was in a room on my own. I knew I couldn't stay there, not because the hospital wouldn't let me, but because people were out to kill me, and staying in one place was going to make it easier for them to do so.

I touched my side gingerly. There was a dressing covering the stitches, so I couldn't see the full extent of the mess I was in, and I was pleased about that. I thought about swinging my legs round and sitting up, but before I had the chance, the door opened, and a male nurse came in.

He looked at me and smiled. "Hello there," he said.

"Hello."

"You gave us quite a scare, Mr..." the nurse paused, waiting for me to fill in my name. That was good. They didn't know who I was.

"Nilsson," I lied.

"It looked like a knife wound," the nurse said. "We were concerned."

"I was cooking. Tripped and fell with it in my hand. It happened so fast."

The nurse looked at me for a moment, and then nodded.

"Accidents will happen," he said. "It should be okay, now. The wound wasn't very deep. If you rest here a few hours, you'll be okay to go."

"Thank you," I said.

The nurse turned to go, then turned back. "Oh, and no cooking for a while."

"Definitely not."

He closed the door and I was alone in the grey room once more. Beside me, my belongings were on a chair. Carefully, I leant forward and, using just my arm muscles, picked up my bag and my jacket. I found my phone and checked the time. Two seventeen AM. I found the charger, plugged it into a socket on the wall, and plugged the other end into the phone. I set my alarm for four AM, lay back and shut my eyes.

*

I dreamed, and this is what I dreamed:

I was in the café drinking tea. Outside, it was light. Not sunny, just light. The sky was white with cloud, and opposite me, where the supermarket should have been, the three huts sat and waited.

I didn't recognise any of the waitresses, yet I knew them all by name. The owner, who wasn't the normal owner, watched me from behind the counter. I had no urgency to leave, but he didn't want me there. He looked up every so often, first at me, and then towards the huts.

A waitress put a plate on my table, even though I didn't remember ordering anything. When I looked at the plate, it was alive with maggots and I recoiled. This was the owner's way to get me to leave.

The door to the café opened and I looked up expecting to see something terrible enter, yet no one was there, no one visible at least. The door closed slowly, and I watched as something unseen made its way towards my table, pushing café furniture out of the way as they approached.

I held my breath as the chair opposite mine was pulled out and then shuffled in. Something was sitting there; I just couldn't see it.

Moments passed. Whatever it was, it was looking at me, sizing me up. I looked at the empty space before me, unwilling to be afraid. Everyone in the café had stopped. They were waiting to see what happened next.

The plate moved slightly, then was pulled slowly across the table.

"Are you her?" I asked. The plate stopped, and a spoon rose unaided before my eyes. Slowly, almost painfully, it scooped the maggots up, into its unseen mouth.

I don't know how my mind works, if it works, when it works. I knew this was a dream. I knew I was making it all up; imagining every detail. Still, I marvelled as the invisible teeth popped each maggot, chewed, and then swallowed them into oblivion.

The horror continued until the plate was almost empty, whereupon it picked the last of the larvae up with its fingers and ate them individually. Then nothing. Nothing moved. Nothing was said. I looked around and everyone in the café was looking at me with hate-filled eyes.

"Hello," I said to my unseen companion. Nothing. "Are you Freya?" The salt cellar was thrown against the floor, smashing it into spiteful shards. "I guess that's a no."

It lifted the pepper pot and I braced myself for another crash. This time, however, it remained above the table, hovering yet not hovering, before being tipped downwards. The pepper fell out with a satisfying 'shhhh' sound, and, as I followed the granules down, I saw the thing was making a pattern on the table. Not just a pattern, but letters, and the letters spelled out a word.

Songström.

"You need me to go to Songström?" I asked. More pepper, more letters.

Yes.

More pepper.

Stand up.

I stood up. The café was gone. The table was gone. I was in the centre of the huts.

The fleeting realisation that it was all a dream visited me. I wanted to wake up, but then it was gone and I knew no better. Here I was in Songström, once more. Always here. It always came back to here.

I looked to the right, and saw the sky had begun to turn red above the buildings; a burning red. It was another warning, but I was beyond warnings. I turned and made my way towards it.

The huts were in the wrong order, and that confused me for a moment. Then I understood; I was approaching them from a different direction. Did that mean anything? Was it something to do with my age?

I moved around the outside of the old woman's hut, across to the furthest, ramshackle one, and stood in front of it. It was in a better condition than the first time I'd visited, the wood less rotten. I blinked. No, not less rotten; not rotten at all. The first hut was now fine.

I walked up the steps and knocked on the door.

"Come in," came a woman's voice. I opened the door. A woman, the barmaid from earlier, stood in the middle of the room, one side of her head shaved, and wearing the same clothes.

"Why aren't you in the bar?" I asked before I could make any sense of it.

"Bar's closed now. Come in. Don't leave the door open."

I entered and shut the door. "Is this where you live?" I asked her.

"I can't afford much on my wages."

"What about the old woman? With the maggots?"

The woman looked at me as if I was mad. "There's no old woman with maggots. No old woman at all. Everyone's young around here."

"This is Songström?"

"Yes. It's not luxury, but what do you expect?"

"I'm looking for my girlfriend."

"You said, earlier. Haven't you found her?"

"I think she's somewhere here. How do you get here?"

"You're asking me whilst standing here yourself."

"This is a dream. I need to find it in the real world."

"Real world?" she asked, the corners of her mouth turning up. "Whenever you visit Songström, it becomes the real world."

72

"How did you get here?" I repeated. I was starting to feel frustrated.

"Do you remember where I worked?"

I nodded. "The bar."

"The truth might be there."

There was a heavy feeling in my stomach. "Are you dead?" I asked her.

"Go and find me and then you will know."

"Why doesn't anyone give me a normal answer!" I shouted.

Her face became instantly angry, her eyes almost murderous. "This is a fucking journey, Sammel!" she screamed at me. "A fucking journey!"

My own anger grew, but there was no need. This was my dream, after all. She couldn't tell me anything I didn't already know. I looked at her for a few moments, then turned and walked out. At the bottom of the steps I stopped and stared at the other huts. Smoke snaked out of Songström's chimney. It hadn't been there before, I was certain. Almost certain. It meant someone was home, someone was waiting for me to knock on the door.

That didn't seem like a good idea. I could hear something else. Windchimes? I couldn't see any on the huts, and Songström wasn't the sort of place for windchimes.

I looked to the sky, where it was red, and now the sky was framed with a window, and an alarm was sounding, bringing me out of my sleep. I looked around. It was the same hospital room they'd put me in earlier, and I was glad to be back.

I waited, seeing how I felt, if I was in pain. I wasn't. In fact, I felt good. I pushed my legs off the bed, stood and dressed. I picked up my bags, and without looking back into the room, left.

*

The rest of the hospital, or at least its corridors, were deserted, and it felt like everyone was avoiding me. Was it possible they knew about Songström? About how it lived inside of me, and they didn't want to catch it? I wanted to shout out; wanted to put my fingers down my throat and retch up anything that would show them I was just another human being with bile inside my stomach.

I didn't, of course. These feelings wash over me, threaten to overtake me, but, more often than not, I'm able to get control of myself and push them away. I wonder if that person, the one who struggles inside to keep control, is the only part of me that's real.

I reached the entrance to the hospital without being challenged, and walked out into the very early morning, feeling alone and frustrated.

In my dream, the barmaid had said to go to the bar where she worked, but it'd be closed now. I didn't want to go back to my flat, either. The flat could be Songström, and I wanted to find Freya, had to find Freya. Time was passing.

I was at a loss, and at these times, when my thoughts needed to be rescued, I knew only one person who could help.

Bobby.

*

When I first started the job at the supermarket, I befriended one of the warehouse workers, a scruffy man by the name of Bobby. I liked Bobby, he was a bit rough around the edges, but he was always someone I could trust.

Bobby lived on his own in a flat near the poor end of town. He squatted there, but whoever the owners were didn't seem bothered by his presence.

My bike was missing, or perhaps the hospital had secured it safely away, so I would have to walk. It'd take a little while, but just having somewhere to aim for, made it easier for my feet to keep going. The pain in my side was all but gone. Garrick's knife really couldn't have gone in very far.

*

The door was open when I got there, so I went in, up the stairs to the first floor, and knocked on his door. There was no answer. I knocked again. Still nothing. I pushed at the door, and like Mrs Garrick's, it swung open.

"Hello!" I called through the gap. "I'm looking for Bobby. Is Bobby here?"

"Who the fuck is it?" came the reply. I smiled. It was Bobby. I felt happy.

"It's Sammel, Bobby. From the supermarket."

There was a pause. "Sammel?"

"Yes."

"From the supermarket?"

"Yes."

"Are you in trouble?"

"Maybe," I said.

A figure shuffled along the hallway and stopped.

"Well, come in then, I can't do everything my fucking self."

*

Bobby had a beard. A black and grey beard, which made it look like he could be the skipper of a boat. He didn't remind me of my father, but he reminded me of a father, and I liked him for it. There was a wisdom about him, one worth paying attention to.

Bobby also used a lot of expletives. I'd quickly learnt to ignore them, but at the supermarket most of the customers avoided him whenever he was working on the shop floor. I thought that was sad.

"Well, you look like three-day-old shit," Bobby said, standing in the small front room in just his boxers. He was a thin man, and I could see each rib. "Want coffee?"

I nodded. I didn't care what it was he was offering, I was just grateful for the kindness.

"Well, I ain't getting it for you. You know where everything is."

Bobby turned and walked away. I cleaned the cups as best I could, and made two coffees with what he had.

When I brought them out, he was sitting, looking out the window. I sat down opposite him.

"You know it's Saturday fucking morning, right?" he asked me.

"I do. I didn't have anywhere else to go."

"Don't you live with someone, Freda, or something?"

"Freya, yes. But she's gone missing."

"Missing? Well, why the fuck did she do that?"

"I'm not sure she had anything to do with it. Something may have happened to her."

Bobby looked at me for a short while. "How long has she been missing?

"Since yesterday. She didn't come back after work. The police found her bag."

"Well, she's not been missing long. Christ, there are whole fucking weeks I can't remember. A day ain't nothing."

"I think something else is happening, Bobby."

"Something else, Sammel?" Bobby looked down, shook his head and sighed. "Like what?"

"I don't know. Nothing makes any sense. Freya's gone, and then there's the Sikkilite, and I'm having really weird dreams. I don't understand what's going on. It's difficult to know how to process it.

I'm worried I'm going mad, Bobby. What if I'm going mad? What if I am mad?"

"Ain't one of us who isn't a little round the twist, Sammel. That's what keeps us alert. Keeps us alive. The truly sane people? They're the fuckers who lost it first. Not us. We just keep going, accepting all the weird shit and fitting it into our lives like it's the most fucking obvious thing ever. So, if you think you're a little crazy, you hang onto it. It makes the whole fucking ride a little easier."

"Thank you."

"What the fuck for?"

"You have a different way of looking at things. It helps."

Bobby looked at me, his hard expression softening a little. "We all grow up differently. I reckon we all have a chance to be anyone when we're younger. Then something happens, and you change because of it. Perhaps if that something hadn't happened, you'd be a different person. Perhaps you'd have been more like me. What do I know? I dunno. I don't really understand any of it. Sometimes I think we're all here to deliver one pearl of wisdom to someone. One act, be it kindness, revenge, love, understanding. We're here to deliver it, and then the rest of our lives are just getting in the way. I feel like I'm getting in the way, Sammel. You ever feel like that?"

I shook my head. "Not yet. I see what you're saying though. We all start out just a single plain puzzle piece and our experiences form the pattern, form the edges, and then God or fate or whatever, it starts looking for the next piece, and lo and behold, they see us, lying at the edge of the board, and we look perfect. We've had the right sort of life, the right sort of experiences, and they pick us up, and they look at us for a moment. For a split second their sole gaze is on us. They turn us around, looking at the edges we've created, looking at our pattern, and they say, 'Yes, you'll do' and that's when we shine; when they look at us. Then we're placed in the puzzle, and that's that. That's our function, and everything else is just waiting for them to finish the picture."

Bobby looked at me for a moment. "You've got a weird fucking brain, Sammel, if you don't mind me saying so."

"I don't mind. I know I have a weird brain."

"Drink your coffee, it looks like you might need it."

I took a couple of sips. It was still hot. "Garrick stabbed me."

"Doesn't surprise me."

"Doesn't it?"

"Garrick's an A-one prick."

"Yes."

"Why did he stab you?"

"He said he was told to. He said they threatened his mother."

"Who did?"

"The person who took the pictures of me. They told Garrick he had to kill me, but he didn't, and when I went to check on his mother, she was already dead. The front of her face, of her skull was missing, and the inside of her head had been scooped out."

"Wow," Bobby said.

"Fucking wow," I said, which made Bobby laugh. I liked that. In all the senselessness of the last twenty-four hours, the fact I'd made Bobby laugh felt like a glimmer of gold in the prospector's pan.

"That's some story," Bobby said, when the laughing stopped.

"It's not a story. It's real. Someone wants me dead."

"And how does that make you feel?"

Sometimes I have to think a long time about something, sometimes I don't. "It makes me feel like I'm about to be placed in that puzzle," I said, almost immediately.

"I bet it does."

I drank both coffees whilst Bobby stared out the window, lost in thought.

"Well?" I asked him.

He steadied his gaze on me. "Do you want to take a shower? You look like you need one."

"If you don't mind."

Bobby smiled. "It's all there. There's a towel in the cupboard, and a clean t-shirt. Knock yourself out."

*

I spent too long in the shower, but it didn't matter. I kept the phone nearby, and checked it every so often for messages. Nothing came through. I dressed in my jeans and Bobby's t-shirt.

When I entered the lounge, Bobby was also dressed.

"Want some toast?" he asked. I did. I went to the kitchen and made it.

I sat down at the table opposite him with my plate, and a thought struck me. Perhaps Bobby was the invisible person from my dream? The one who ate the maggots.

"I'm going to help you," he said.

"Are you?"

"Yes."

"Why?"

"Because I'm not prepared to be put in the puzzle just yet."

I nodded. "Me neither."

Bobby smiled, but there was some sadness in his eyes. "My boy," he said. "You might just be the whole fucking puzzle."

*

After the toast, Bobby said, "We need to go to the supermarket."

"Why?"

"Because of Garrick. We need to speak to Garrick. Little prick might know more than he's letting on. I might be able to get the information from him."

"And if he doesn't know anything?"

"Who cares?"

Something had changed in Bobby. A little pilot light had been reignited deep inside of him, ready to flare at any moment.

"Now, get a little sleep before we go. No need to be exhausted before we get there."

"I'm not tired," I said.

"Just get some fucking sleep."

*

When I next opened my eyes the clock above Bobby's mantelpiece read seven o'clock. For a moment, I thought I was alone again, that he had taken off whilst I was asleep, but then he cleared his throat from nearby.

"Perhaps Freda fucking left you because of all the snoring," he said.

"Freya," I corrected him.

"Whatever. I think we need to order a taxi to the supermarket. You got any cash?"

I nodded. "Lots."

*

The sky was lighter as we travelled in the back of the taxi. I thought it might make everything better, but it didn't. Bad people walked in the daylight, too. All the daylight did was hide them amongst everyone else. I felt my chest tightening, and I breathed deeply and slowly to counteract it.

*

The store opened at seven-thirty, and by then we were waiting outside. I wasn't sure Garrick would turn up. I expected he would have found his mother by now, so he'd either be at the police station, or in shock.

At seven thirty-six AM, however, he appeared. He walked as he always had, leaning slightly back with broad strides, as if he was being chased but was afraid to admit it.

He unlocked the door and pushed it open. As soon as he had, Bobby and I were there behind him.

"What's this about?" Garrick said.

"Just get the fuck inside. I want to ask you a few questions."

"About what?"

"Not here. In your office."

*

"I should ring the police," Garrick hissed, when we were all cramped into his room.

"And say what? We've done nothing a boy in blue is going to bother themselves about."

"This is private property."

Bobby laughed.

"Fuck you. Stab anyone lately?"

"No," Garrick said.

The human mind's a wonderful beast. It notices a great many things it shouldn't be able to. Like the nanosecond that was the

83

difference between Garrick's reply being the truth and it being a lie. It was a lie. Both myself and Bobby could tell. Garrick could tell, too.

Bobby was losing his patience.

"Sit down, and show me the knife."

"There isn't a knife."

Garrick was beginning to sweat.

"Get me the knife, or I'll find it, and so help me God, I'll stick it in you."

There are many heroes in the world. Sometimes I saw the news, and in the café, I often read the front of other people's newspapers. Heroes did amazing things, but they also did small things. They stood up for people that didn't deserve it. People like me. At that moment, in the security office, Bobby was truly being a hero for me. He believed in me, when no one else would.

Garrick used a shaky hand to point a shaky finger at the bottom drawer in his desk.

"Open it."

He leant forward and slowly pulled it open. In the bottom of the drawer was the knife, with my blood still on it.

Bobby looked at me. "What the fuck?" he said.

"Why did someone threaten to kill me? Why didn't you go to the police?"

Garrick was silent then. He didn't want to tell us, but he didn't have to. Perhaps it was the coffee I'd drunk at Bobby's, perhaps not, either way my brain had instantly worked it out. He didn't go to the police, because it was the police.

"Fuck," Bobby said. "What are we getting ourselves into, Sammel?"

I didn't reply, because I didn't know. Instead I looked at Garrick. "What about your mother?" I asked him.

"What about her?"

"I saw her, last night. She was dead."

"Well, for a dead person, she was very perky this morning."

This time, Garrick was telling the truth. He was grinning at me like I was an idiot.

"But she was sitting in her chair when I saw her," I explained. "And her face was missing."

"Nope. She was fine when I got back. Doped up on medication. Asleep in the armchair."

I tried to think back to last night. I had been surprised there hadn't been more blood, but I was certain what I'd seen hadn't been a trick of the light. I had seen the back of her skull. I should have taken a picture. Bobby put his hand on my shoulder.

"You all right?" he asked.

I nodded, then turned to Garrick. "I'm glad she's..." I started, but didn't know how to finish it.

"I don't want you to visit us again," Garrick said. "We're going away for a few weeks. Let everything die down."

"Wait a minute," I said. "You stabbed me. You can't just lie low."

"What do you think is going to happen if you report it, Sammel? Who the hell do you think is first in the chain of command?"

He was right. There wasn't anything we could do.

"We better go," Bobby said. "Too much weird shit going on here."

*

We sat in the café opposite the supermarket. I checked my phone. No messages.

"You're not exactly Mr Popular," Bobby said.

"I was hoping Freya might have messaged."

Bobby sighed. He was about to say something I wouldn't like. "Listen, Sammel, I need to ask you a question."

"Okay."

"When you saw Garrick's mother last night, were you high?"

"Quite high. He lives above a shop."

"You know, I'd laugh if I thought you meant to tell a joke. I mean drugs. Had you been taking drugs?"

"No. I don't take drugs anymore."

"Anymore? What sort of drugs did you used to take?"

"I don't know what they were for. I used to get them from the doctor's."

"Medication?"

"Yes, medication."

"No recreational drugs?"

"No. You think I might have been hallucinating?"

"There aren't many other explanations that don't end up with you wrapped up like a present in a padded cell."

"I was worried about that," I said.

"So, any previous history of hallucinating? With you, or your family?"

I took a deep breath. "Have I ever told you about my mother?"

"You've never mentioned either of your parents. I assumed you fell out of a stork's cradle one day. Landed on your head."

"Not quite," I said.

*

My mother used to have visions, though they were nearly always brought on by the consumption of alcohol. If you didn't monitor her drinking, or didn't find the stash she'd hidden in her room, you could almost guarantee the appearance of something weird every single night. Everyone put it down to the alcohol. I put it down to the alcohol.

Her visions were not unlike what I'd experienced with Garrick's mother. She would call them 'demons', and claimed she saw them everywhere. Whenever she started discussing them my father would get a look on his face. That look, I now understood, was one of desperation. He was losing her; that was what he thought.

But, my God, she might have been right. If all the things I kept seeing weren't demons, then what the hell were they? And as I hadn't had any alcohol to act as a stimulus, I couldn't simply write them off as products of my inebriation.

Yet, how could they be real?

In the end, my mother committed suicide. It was her way out.

That's not the whole story. I try and forget the whole story.

*

Bobby sat quietly and listened. I didn't tell him about Songström, or the dream with the waitress. I had to let him in slowly. He was helping me, but if he thought I was too far gone, he might leave, write me off as a lost cause.

"Fuck," he said, when I'd finished.

"What do you think we should do next?"

"We've got to find Freya. If we can find her, then a lot of this 'holy crap weird shit' stuff goes away. We can put some stuff into context."

I laughed.

"What's the matter?"

"I've never heard you say the word context, before."

"Fuck off."

*

We got a taxi back to my flat, and stood on the pavement looking up at the windows.

"Are we just going to fucking stand here?" Bobby asked.

I shrugged. I didn't know. The flat looked normal from the outside, but what would we find beyond the front door? I wanted my flat to be Songström because then I wouldn't have to explain it to Bobby, and I didn't want my flat to be Songström because I didn't want to go back there.

Mostly, though, I didn't want to be mad, like my mother, but perhaps it was inevitable. Perhaps my mental health had been written the day I was born. I felt like crying. I didn't want something to be wrong with me. I wanted to be all right.

We crossed the road to the flats, climbed the stairs and walked the length of the corridor until we were standing by my door. It was locked. I retrieved the key from my bag and placed it in the mechanism.

Bobby put his hand on my wrist. "I know this is difficult," he said.

I nodded that I understood, twisted the key and the handle, and nudged open the door.

"Freya?" I called. "It's Sammel. Are you there?"

There wasn't any answer. I pushed the door wider. It wasn't Songström. It was the flat. The flat as I remembered leaving it. I walked into the hallway, Bobby staying close behind me.

"I'll just check our bedroom," I told him. "The lounge is through there."

I went to the bedroom door, and pushed it open. The bed was made. Beside the bed was the book I was reading. Just how I left it. Freya's side of the bed was neat and tidy. It didn't look like she'd been back. I walked out of the hallway and went into the bathroom. Nothing had moved position. Not the toothbrush nor hairbrush nor deodorant. Nothing.

I walked down the hallway to the lounge. Bobby was standing in the centre of it looking around. He shook his head at me to indicate he hadn't found her.

"Did you look in the kitchen?" I asked. He shook his head again.

It was one door further up the hall. I checked it. Empty.

Bobby pushed past, walked up to the fridge, and took the little magnetic notepad off it.

"What the fuck is this?" he asked.

"It's where Freya writes the shopping list."

Bobby looked at me. "You work in a supermarket, and you let your girlfriend do the shopping?"

"She likes doing it," I said.

"Yeah, right," Bobby grumbled. "Where's your bathroom?"

"First door as you came in."

I watched him leave, then went back to the lounge, to the table by the window. I tipped Freya's bag upside down, and watched the contents spill out. There was a lot there, so I spent a little time arranging everything so it could all be seen.

I stared at them until Bobby came out of the bathroom. He coughed from the doorway, and I realised I hadn't moved for a while. Outside, the sky had grown dark, and my legs ached.

"You zoned out there, Sammel," he said,

"It happens sometimes."

Bobby came closer. "Is that her stuff?"

"Everything in her handbag."

Bobby stepped closer to the table and ran his hand over some of her belongings.

"Women need a few more fucking pockets, if you ask me," he said. "Do you recognise any of it?"

"What?"

"Well, just what I said. It's not fucking hard. Do you recognise any of it?"

I looked at the objects laid out. I tried to imagine her with them. Holding them. I tried to remember her hand. Her arms, her body. I tried to remember Freya. I got nothing.

"I'm not sure what she looks like, Bobby. I'm not sure she exists. I'm sorry. This might all be for nothing."

I went and sat on the couch.

"Let's get one thing straight," Bobby said. "I'm helping you because the police told someone to kill you. And if they did that, then something's definitely happening, whether you hallucinated your girlfriend or not. And even if you did, hell, I'm sure you're not the first."

"Maybe."

"So, we need to find Freya, or at least work out who she is, but not because she's in any kind of trouble, but because your life is in danger, and she might know something about it. Okay?"

"Okay."

"Where was the handbag found?"

"Near the train station."

"So, why the fuck aren't we near the train station?"

"I don't know."

"Sammel, you really are..." Bobby began, but then stopped. "Where'd that come from?" he asked, pointing beside me. I looked and saw a cushion, the one from the hut. The one with the steam train on it.

I tried to twist my head back around to tell Bobby to go, but something was stopping me. I tried to open my mouth, but it wouldn't open. Then I felt the pressure, first on the top of my head, and then below my chin, like something was holding my head, and twisting it.

"What's happening?" Bobby said, but I couldn't tell him.

I raised my hands to my head to try to stop it from being twisted off my neck.

Bobby walked into my view, and looked at me. I tried to convey with my eyes that I was in trouble.

I glanced over to the cushion, but it was no longer a cushion. It was the bottom half of the old woman's body. It stopped at the waist, but it occurred to me that it was her who was trying to kill me.

I moved my eyes up and down to indicate the cushion.

"Motherfucker! Who's that?" Bobby shouted.

Without hesitation, he reached down, grabbed the woman's legs, and pulled.

"She won't move," he said. "It's like she's made of fucking concrete!"

He thumped her legs a few times, and stamped on her feet. Nothing seemed to be working. The pressure was increasing on my head, and I thought it was going to beat me. She was going to snap my neck like a twig.

Bobby lifted a chair up and brought it down where the woman's torso would be. The pressure on my head shifted.

I managed to squeeze out the words, "Do it!"

Bobby heard, and brought the chair down once more. Another shift. Then Bobby was repeatedly hitting the sofa, and the pressure gradually released, until it was gone.

She was gone.

"What the fuck just happened?" Bobby asked.

"It was her. The woman from Songström."

"What the fucking hell is Songström?"

"It's something else I need to explain."

I looked down to where the woman and the cushion had been. There was nothing.

"We have to get out of here, now," I said.

"Already fucking on it."

Bobby grabbed my arm, and pulled me out of the flat. We descended the stairs and exited the building without looking back.

*

Outside the air was cool, purifying. We'd made it. Somehow, we'd kept Songström at bay. I wanted to shout, to whoop. Instead, I put my head down, tried not to throw up and followed Bobby as quickly as possible.

We hadn't gone very far before we noticed the blue flashing light of a police car off in the distance, behind us.

"They're coming for me," I whispered to Bobby.

"Don't worry," he replied. "I'll go, try and distract them. You get to the station as quickly as possible. We'll meet up later."

"It's dangerous. The police are dangerous."

"Well, I'm fucking dangerous. Leave this to me."

I felt the pressure on my arm release and Bobby was gone. I ducked down a side street, and kept walking until I felt far enough away from my flat.

I stopped to get my breath. The night was cool and I had to reach the railway station. Without my bicycle, the journey could take an hour, and I didn't want to be out on the streets for that long; didn't want to waste the time, or risk the exposure.

I found my phone, checked for messages, and then dialled the taxi firm. I still had a lot of money on me, more than enough for a cab ride.

"Where'd you like to go?" the woman on the line asked. She sounded bored. I didn't blame her.

"The station," I replied.

"I think you've probably missed the last train."

"I don't want to catch a train."

A slight pause; a pause that indicated she thought I was a crank caller.

"Then why do you want to go to the station? There's nothing else out there."

"I'm meeting someone. Is that okay with you?"

The line went quiet whilst she decided what to do. After a moment, I heard her sigh. "Where do you want picking up from?"

I looked at the road name. "Beech Way."

"A car will be there in five minutes," she said, and ended the call.

*

95

I stood alone amongst the unknown houses, wondering about the lives going on behind their walls, behind their windows. I wanted to go up to the doors and knock on them, tell the owners they didn't own the house, no one owned them. They were just shells that people hid behind until they died, or broke free, whichever came first. I wanted to tell them I could help them break free. I could break their houses, break their shells, and they could see the world as it truly was; full of horror.

I wanted to shout at them, to scream and convince them in any way possible to let go. A darkness fell over me, and I began to feel hopeless and frightened. There wasn't anything I could do. The waters had come and there was nothing I could do. I closed my eyes against the doors and windows, and breathed slowly. I had to get myself back under control.

If only I could understand this life I'd been given. I wondered how anyone coped with it. Most of the day I was lost in a sea of information, and it took everything I had not to curl up into a corner and weep.

I thought of Freya.

Thinking of Freya always made me think more clearly. She would tell me to see things as she saw them, and she'd tell me what she saw, and what she thought of things. I could see it, then, through her eyes. She would tell me how she saw the world, and it would all make sense.

Freya wasn't there, though, and my mind continued to spiral. I wanted to sit down, bury my head in my hands. I looked for a wall to lean on, but all of them had sharp prongs to stop me. They didn't want me there. Not on their street, not on Beech Way. I heard the growling noise I made when I started to lose control. Low and guttural. I moaned, and the moan stopped the growl but only for a moment.

Too many doors, too many people. They thought, and thought, and I didn't know what they were thinking, and they were thinking about me, about how stupid I was, about how I didn't understand how walking down the street couldn't be filled with confusion. They weren't looking at me. They didn't want to look at me. Just think about me, and thinking about me was worse. Their thoughts crawled through the air, crawled into my ears, tried to take over my mind.

I was losing control, and they knew it because that's what they wanted. They wanted me to lose control, to shout, to scream. They wanted me to cry and kick and punch and I couldn't be me anymore, and when I wasn't me I didn't know who I was and I needed to get out and I needed to hit out and I needed to scream at the top of my lungs and I needed Freya.

"Ssshhh," came a voice behind me. "Take my hands, and see things as I do."

"You're not there, you've gone. You didn't come home and you've gone."

"I'm behind you. Take my hands and see things through my eyes."

I closed my eyes, turned and held my arms out. I felt her cool hands slip into mine, and it was wonderful.

"This is what I see," Freya said, her voice like medicine. "I see an empty street. Empty but for a man who's looking for someone he lost, and he's doing well, so well. The others are out to get you, and you must be better than them. Cleverer than them. That's what they fear the most. They fear you staying in control, so they will try to scare you, but you mustn't be scared. You are a strong man, a kind man, who shows his love in many ways. The car will pick you up and take you to the station. You must be pleasant to the man, whatever he says, however he tries to goad you. No one is your friend, but you have to be stronger than them. Do you think you can do that?"

"Yes, Freya," I said.

"Are you back in control?"

"I am back in control."

"The car is nearly here. You must get to the station. You must not stop your quest to find me, whatever stands in your way. There's a reason why I chose you, Sammel. Draw strength from that. Be my hero."

"I will."

Then the hands slipped out of mine and I knew she had gone. I opened my eyes. Freya had found me, from wherever she was, she had found me and calmed me down.

As I looked into the space I imagined she'd been standing in, a set of headlights turned the corner and approached. I could see the yellow taxi sign on the top of the car. It pulled over.

"Sammel?" the man said. I nodded.

"I'm Sammel."

"I'm your lift to the station."

I opened the back door and got in.

"Everything okay?" the taxi driver said.

I nodded. "Yes. Just having one of those days."

"You should try driving a taxi. Those days are every damn day."

"I can imagine."

He laughed gently, as the car pulled away from the kerb.

*

"So, off to the station then?" he asked.

"Yes."

"I didn't know trains ran this late."

"They don't. I'm meeting someone, that's all."

"Sounds very clandestine."

"Yes," I said, though I wasn't sure what clandestine meant. "Have you been driving long?"

"About five years," he replied. "I got made redundant, and couldn't do much else. So much for 'a job for life'."

"Yes." I thought about the supermarket. I never thought of that as a job for life. I had never really known what I was going to do. "Do you enjoy it?"

"Some days. Some days it's better to just get in the car and drive people where they want to go. At least you're making someone happy. Everything else might be going to shit, pardon the expression, but you're able to make someone's life easier. On those days, I welcome the job. Then there are the other days, where I'm sorely tempted to simply drive over a cliff. Or stall it on a level crossing when the gates are going down. Do you know what I mean?"

I nodded. "Days when being dead just means you've nothing to worry about anymore. I understand."

"Lived here long?" he asked.

"A few years. That's all."

"I've lived here all my life. Seen things I love been torn away or torn down. You don't want to stay in the same place for too long. Stay in one place and people take advantage of you. Like you're a public toilet or something. Yeah, that works. People shit on you, pardon the expression, if you hang around too long."

"I won't be here much longer," I said to him. "There's nothing here for me anymore."

The driver adjusted his rear-view mirror, and I felt his eyes on me.

"You're not thinking of doing anything stupid, are you? 'Cause I don't want to be telling police how you seemed such a normal person, and I had no idea you were going to commit suicide. I don't want to be driving you to your death. That wouldn't be a good start to the week."

"I've no intention of killing myself for at least a little while. That okay?"

He paused a moment. "Yeah, that'll do."

Outside, the streetlights thinned out, then disappeared altogether. It was dark inside the taxi. The driver kept quiet, gently tapping on the steering wheel to a tune that only played in his head.

"Shit, I wouldn't want to be out here," he said as the station approached. "You sure you're meeting someone?"

"Yeah, I'm sure," I lied.

"You got a torch? You're going to need a torch."

"I've got my phone."

"How much battery you got left?"

"Not much. Never have much anymore."

The numbers on the taxi meter continued to creep up. I had the money.

I looked out the window and a thought struck me.

"It's dark," I said.

"What? You shitting me? Pardon the expression."

"I was standing at the window in my flat. I was looking out and... Christ, how long was I looking out the window for?"

The driver shook his head. "Can't tell you that, I'm afraid. Perhaps you had something on your mind."

"Perhaps."

I sat there, being jostled by the ride, trying to remember the sky turning from light to dark.

"Here we are," he said, pulling into the station car park. I was beginning to feel anxious again.

"Thank you," I said, giving him the money for the ride, and some extra for a tip. He watched as I got out of the idling car. Before I'd had chance to walk away, he wound his window down, and held out something in a gloved hand.

"Take this," he said. It took a moment for my eyes to adjust. He was holding a torch, heavy and black. "The battery will last a while, and if you get any trouble, it'll be pretty effective against a skull, if you know what I mean."

"I do." I took the torch. "I'll get it back to the taxi firm. Who should I tell them it's for?"

"Berg," the taxi driver said. "Berg should be fine."

I stood and watched the car drive away. Berg had been a nice man. He had leant me his torch. I switched it on and shone it at the floor. It was very bright.

"Good," I said.

I'd been to the station on several occasions, but it all looked different in the dark. It occurred to me, as I stood there, that our perception of the world was based entirely on its lighting conditions, on the information we were given, and how we interpreted it.

The station was closed, that was for sure. The padlock on the door to the ticket office wasn't going to budge. Not that I thought I needed to get into that part of the station. The bag was found near it, after all. I scanned the surrounding area, making sweeps with the torch beam. There were three cars in the car park. Why any cars should be there was a mystery at first, but then I realised the owners were probably staying away for the night, and coming back tomorrow, or the next day.

Around the car park's edge was a fence of metal, about shoulder height. On one side lay the platform and tracks, to the left and right were woods, and finally, on the last side, the one opposite the station, was the road I'd come in on.

I crouched down by the station entrance and opened my bag. I was getting hungry, and I usually carried a couple of cereal bars in a plastic container.

I found them and sat down on the steps. As I ate the first one, I played with the torch a little, and found another setting which made the light dimmer. I set it to that. It wasn't great, but it was okay, and I figured the longer the battery lasted, the better.

I finished the cereal bar, and put the wrapper back in the container. Litter had always angered me. The idea that people liked to see the world with tiny pieces of misplaced colour made my fingers itch.

I had to think about where I should start looking first. There was too much ground to cover by randomly searching. Someone probably found her bag in the car park or on the platform. That seemed more likely than stumbling over it in the woods. No one in their right mind would be walking in the woods at any time of the day.

I had a feeling I was missing something else, something important, something obvious, but I didn't have time to sit around and wait for whatever it was to appear in my mind. I had to get going. Time was ticking by.

I stood and went to the platform; it had less ground to cover than the car park. When the ticket office was closed, they opened a gate to the side, which led to platform one. To get across to the other platform you went up and over the tracks via an old wooden bridge.

The platforms were surprisingly long. They fitted a twelve-carriage train, which was odd because the town didn't have that many commuters. Perhaps it had been busier in the past. Perhaps they had overdone the design.

Platform One ran, if you were a train, northwards. It consisted of five benches, two signs, the waiting room, and the toilets. There were no buildings on the other platform whatsoever.

All the lights were off. It made sense, but still felt strange. I turned right, walking parallel to the platform edge, and shone my dimmed torch around as I made my way along. Nothing looked out of place. I peered through the door to the ticket office from this side. There was a cover pulled down over where you bought tickets, and a rack on the wall, which held assorted leaflets, five of which were slightly askew.

Nothing seemed strange, though it was an odd room, really. A room where no one stopped, no one looked. It was a forgotten place, which looked even more forgotten at night. If it was to have a feeling, I think it would be anger. I think anger stirred in its forgotten corners, and I decided it was best to move on.

The waiting room was next. I tried the door, and whilst if wasn't padlocked, it didn't budge. Inside, I could see sofas, a rug and a cabinet filled with second-hand books people could take if they donated a small amount of money to charity.

There was a sound behind me. One rock knocking another, far enough away not to immediately worry. I turned and shone the torch that way, flicking the setting to high beam for a moment. On the other side of the platform, on the other side of the wire fence, more trees stood. I couldn't see anything. I hadn't expected to see anything.

I turned the torch back to the waiting room door. The small pane of glass next to the handle had been smashed. I didn't know why I hadn't seen it before. The torch was now on high beam, but I'd have thought I'd have seen it. I put my hand in the gap, being careful not to cut myself, and reached down towards the lock. There was a catch mechanism that turned and unlocked the door from within. I twisted it, and the door opened inwards. Carefully, I brought my hand out.

*

The waiting room smelt of old leather, because that's what the sofas were made from. I assumed they must have been donated by someone wealthy, because I'd never seen such luxury at any other station. There was a disused fireplace, which housed a rack with more leaflets, and the bookcase. The floor was made of an uninteresting laminated wood.

The waiting room felt safe. I pushed the door shut and heard the click of the latch. I closed my eyes and breathed in and out a few times; I hadn't felt this safe since Freya went missing, and probably since a long time before it.

*

After Songström, my family moved to a different town. I tried to pretend everything was all right, that the experience hadn't altered me, but my parents began to receive phone calls from my school advising them of my bad behaviour.

My father would say he was doing his best, that things were difficult at home with my mother, and that he'd try and 'sort me out'. The fourth time he was called, he wrote a letter to the education authority telling them I was going to be home-tutored, and we walked to the post box and he lifted me up so I could post it myself. I felt better after that. School had become impossible to understand.

They didn't acknowledge the letter. I just stayed at home, and no one cared about it anymore. My mother kept to her room, so I mostly interacted with my father. He still had a full-time job, still had to pay for the house we were renting, so in the evenings he'd work out some lessons for me to do the next day, and then, over breakfast, he'd talk me through what he wanted me to do. He made the studying fun, and he made sure I was outside for at least an hour a day, whether it was wet or dry.

When I was outside, neighbours would often stop and ask me how I was doing. They'd offer help, and I would suggest they talk to my father. One of these people, a girl named Livia, visited after school every day to make my mother a cup of coffee, and to make me some toast. Livia was nice. She talked a lot, both to me, when she arrived, and to my mother when she took her the coffee.

Livia was four years older than me, with brown hair and brown eyes. She had dimples, which I'd never really seen on anyone before, and didn't know what they were called. It made me want to try and make her smile, though, just so I could see them. There were times when, after she'd come down from seeing my mother, she'd pull out a chair from the small table in the kitchen and she'd say, "Can I look at your work today?" and I'd nod and push whatever book it was I'd been writing in, over to her.

She'd read it in her head, and nod. There must have been problems with it, spelling or grammar, but she never used to mention them. She'd just point out the bits she liked, and then ask me what I was going to write next. She would stay until my father came home, and then she'd leave, walking the short distance to her house. She was very nice, and she made me feel safe.

On her last visit to the house, my mother stabbed her in the arm with a fork. It was a self-defence wound, because she had actually wanted to stab Livia in the eye, both eyes, because my mother said that Livia wore a mask, and the only real part of her face were her eyes. I remember the scream, the movement upstairs. I hadn't waited to find out what was going on, I was on the stairs before the noise had died away, bounding to the top and running through the bedroom door.

Livia had been on her back on the floor, my mother on top of her, screaming and trying to stab her with the fork. Livia was doing her best to fend her off, deflecting every blow as best she could. Blood was smeared on her arm where the fork had struck her, and the side of Livia's face was red. There were tears, too, wetting the girl's cheeks, but she wasn't crying.

I picked up the lamp from beside the bed, and brought it down on my mother's head. She slumped and rolled off immediately, leaving Livia looking confused. Then she saw me with the lamp, scrambled to her feet, grabbed my arm and ran me out of the room, shutting the door behind us.

We didn't stay in the house. We ran out the front door and along the road to where Livia lived. Her mother was in, and as soon as she answered the door, we were ushered into the lounge. Her mother picked up the phone and started dialling different people; first the police, then the ambulance, then her husband, and lastly, my father.

I kept telling Livia I was sorry about what had happened, and asking if she was okay. She told me to stop being so stupid, that it wasn't my fault. She held onto her arm the whole time, where my mother had stabbed her. I remember her father coming back and putting me on the sofa and telling me to rest. I asked to see my father, and they said he'd be there when I woke.

I fell asleep quickly, the tiredness inside expanding and making me heavy. I yawned a couple of times, closed my eyes and dreamed.

*

My mother was with me and we were on an island in the middle of a bay. Around the edge of the bay, standing where the sand met the sea were the monsters. They watched us and they wanted us. My mother held my hand, and she said I had to be brave, that if I was brave I might survive.

I looked at her and asked her what she meant. She said everything was going to be okay. That I could defeat them; defeat the demons on the edge of the water. The trick is not to let them know you knew. I had to keep it quiet. If I let them know then the same thing that happened to her would happen to me. I asked her what that was.

She squeezed my hand, and started to walk into the water. I asked her where she was going. I asked her not to go. She turned and she told me she was going to cool off, that things were getting hot. She told me to watch out for them; that they were everywhere. She told me she was sorry. She told me she was proud of me.

*

When I woke, there were flashing blue lights and more people in Livia's house than there had been when I'd closed my eyes. I sat up, scared. Livia saw me and came and held my arm. I asked where my father was, and she said she'd go and get him. I nodded and watched her leave.

I was scared then. Scared from my dream. Scared for my mother.

110

My father appeared through the doorway, and he was in tears. He came and he hugged me so hard I knew something bad had happened. I didn't ask. My father was crying, and though he was crying he was telling me everything was going to be all right. He told me he wouldn't let any harm come to me. He told me he would make everything okay.

We were escorted from Livia's house out the back door, through the gate at the end of the garden, and away from where we lived. I asked to be picked up, and in his grief my father did so. I looked over his shoulder towards our house, where the flames licked the sky like a giant bonfire; a bonfire shaped like our house. And out of the window, waving at me, was my mother.

You wouldn't have been able to recognise her; her body was black and charred from the fire. But it was her, and she waved at me and I waved back. I understood what she meant about going into the water to cool off. She was okay.

I glanced down and saw Livia standing at her back garden gate, looking at me. I smiled at her as best I could, but I was cold inside. She waved back and I think I fooled her into believing I was all right. I must have done, for I wouldn't have lasted this long had she suspected otherwise.

As she waved to me, her hand reached up and gripped the place she'd been stabbed, but it was too late, I'd already seen that there was no mark there. She had been stabbed, but in a matter of hours the stab mark had completely disappeared.

*

The train station waiting room was quiet.

I sat on the sofa furthest from the door, and from this position I looked straight out onto the platform. The sofa was surprisingly comfortable, probably due to the number of people who'd used the room before me. My brain started to try and work out how many people that would be, but I pushed the figures away. I had enough to deal with as it was.

Somewhere inside my mind, I wondered if anyone had ever thrown up on the sofa, urinated on it, or even, I supposed, died on it.

People died anywhere. I didn't exactly study the obituaries, but I didn't ignore them, either. Dying doesn't choose a destination, or a time, or a place. Unless you take your own life or kill someone. I expected many people had died at or near the station. I imagined that simply building the railway had been hazardous enough.

There were ghosts, like the ones I saw after I fell off my bicycle. I'd seen them before, not all the time, but when they wanted to remind me they were there. I'm not sure they were specific people. I think, moreover, they're collections of people. So, if enough people die in a similar spot, they can amalgamate into something. A lot of the time it's hate. Hate seems to attract them. I can't really blame them, they're dead, after all. I'd be pretty hateful if I'd died.

Some of them were different, though. Some of them could be made of other emotions, like love, greed or fear. These ghosts are harder to predict. You know what you're getting from hatred, but from greed, well, it's up to the ghost.

I'd never tried calling one before. Who would? It's scary enough when they appear by themselves. Yet I was in a safe place, and I thought that might protect me a little. Of course, I didn't know how to call one, having never done it before, and as I sat on the sofa in the silent waiting room I realised how very little I knew.

I turned the torch off, put it on the table and cleared my throat. There was something plugged into the wall with a small red LED light on it. I hadn't noticed it till now. Even a little light can shine a lot in the darkness.

"Um," I said, which I immediately regretted. It didn't sound like the right way to begin talking to the dead. "My name is Sammel Ahlberg, and I would like to speak with you." That was better. I waited. Nothing happened.

"I'm searching for Freya, who may have been murdered near here. It's important I find her. Can you help?" Again, I listened in the empty room. There were hardly any sounds at all, bar the squeaking of the sofa as I moved.

"I only have a few days to find her. I have a Sikkilite."

There was a noise then. A scratching. I remained silent.

"Sikkilite, you say?" came a deep voice. It sounded like they were sitting next to me, and I very nearly became part of the group who'd urinated on the sofa.

"Yes, Sikkilite. Do you know of it?"

"Who amongst the dead doesn't know of the stone that can keep them safe? They would be a very poor ghost indeed."

"Can you help me find her?"

"I can, but there will be a charge."

I laughed then. I couldn't help it. "I'm sorry," I said to the room. "I didn't mean to laugh."

"You are speaking with a ghost, you are allowed to laugh."

He didn't sound hateful, or fearful. Greedy perhaps, or possibly loving.

"What sort of charge do you ask for?"

"It is very simple. I help you find her, and you give me the Sikkilite."

"I'm not sure it's mine to give."

"Believe me when I say the person who gives it is always the one who took it in the first place. It's an equation, and it always balances."

I nodded. Give and take I could understand.

"Okay," I told the ghost. "I will give you the Sikkilite, if you help me save Freya."

"Deal. I'd shake your hand, but, well, you know."

"I know. What do I call you?"

"I've not had much need for a name up till now. However, you can call me Akono."

"Are there other ghosts around here, Akono?"

"Oh, yes," he said. "And they're all very interested in you."

*

Akono's voice was in my head. He was a ghost, after all, and ghosts don't have voice boxes, or throats, or any of the other important things needed to produce sounds. I didn't know if I could trust him. I was certain Freya would not let me give the Sikkilite away, but the fact of the matter was I had little choice other than to agree to his demands.

"Do you know where she is?" I asked Akono.

"I do not. But what I can tell you is, she is not in this waiting room."

"No," I agreed. I stood, turned the torch back on and walked to the door. "We should look for her. The sooner, the better."

"Yes."

I opened the door and shivered.

"Left or right?" I asked Akono.

"I don't know."

"You're supposed to help me. That's the deal."

"I think we should try the woods," he said.

115

"Why the woods?"

"Because it's not here."

*

The ground was dry. We crossed the car park, passing the cars waiting patiently for their owners like neglected dogs. In front of us, a tall mast had been erected to improve cell phone signals. It was a strange thing to see looming out of the darkness. Like a statue to a deity. I supposed some would say that was exactly what it was.

There was a hole in the fence, neatly snipped and folded back. I bent, turned sideways, and moved through, careful not to cut my hands on the exposed wire.

I walked into the woods, looking at the floor, sweeping the torch first one way and then the other, looking for patterns that shouldn't be there. I hated doing it. I hated looking for Freya as if she was already dead. I stopped.

"What's the matter?" Akono asked.

"It's difficult. I don't want to find her."

"She might not be here."

"And she might be. Perhaps I ought to leave and not come back. It's what I do. It's actually something I'm good at."

"I think you should give it a little more time. I'm sure she would have done the same for you."

"That's just it," I told the ghost. "I'm not so sure she would."

*

I had at least three other homes before I finally settled in this town.

My mother's suicide, for that was how it was referred to, left my father a shell. He stopped his job. Stopped setting the schoolwork. He even stopped feeding me. That was okay. I knew how to feed myself.

We went to her funeral and stood next to each other, but he didn't hold my hand. That's the main thing I remember. He didn't hold my hand.

Livia and her parents were there. They stood on the other side of the coffin with their heads bowed, playing the part of the grieving neighbours. They were very convincing, and after the casket was lowered into the hole, they came around and shook first my father's hand, and then mine. I pretended I hadn't seen Livia's arm the day my mother died. It was for the best. If these people were demons, if what my mother said was true, they were far cleverer and stronger than me.

I watched them, though. At the wake, which was held at their house, I watched them. I heard people talking about me, saying how I hadn't shown any emotion since her death, but what was I supposed to do? It made no sense. My mother had died, and now she wasn't here anymore. Crying wouldn't make it any better, it wouldn't make her come back. Besides, for the best part of a year she'd been shut in her room. I'd lost touch with her.

117

There were more people at the wake then there'd been at the funeral. Most of the people I didn't know, and if they weren't staring at me, they were staring at my father, who sat in a corner with a bottle of wine and no glass. In a way, it was a fitting send-off to my mother, whom I'd often seen in a similar position, drinking red wine from a bottle, trickles of what could have been dark blood falling down her chin.

I missed my mother most then. When I saw the wine. I missed her because she was missing this, and she'd have liked it. I still didn't cry. Instead, I went and sat in Livia's conservatory, a small room with wicker furniture and overstuffed cushions. I sat there and looked out onto the back garden and wondered how everything had gone so wrong.

Livia came in and sat next to me. She wore a dark green dress, with a swirly pattern that shone when she twisted in a certain way.

"Hello," she said, and it sounded like she meant it.

"Hello," I replied.

"I'm sorry about your mother."

"I'm sorry about your arm," I replied. "Is it okay?" I didn't look at her. I didn't want to make too much of it. She shrugged, pulled the sleeve of her dress up and showed me the plaster there. It had three small pinpricks of blood. It looked very effective.

"It itches a bit," she said. "And they tell me I can't scratch it, but I scratch it anyway."

I remained quiet for a long, stretched-out moment. Livia was shifting in her seat, feeling uncomfortable. As she was about to get up I turned to her and said, "Are you afraid of dying, Livia?"

The look of horror on her face was incredible and absolute.

"What?" she asked, her voice raspy.

"Are you afraid of dying?"

"Why do you ask that?"

"I don't know. This is my mother's funeral. What else is there to talk about other than death?"

"Of course I'm afraid of dying," she said. "Aren't you?"

I shook my head. "No, not anymore," I told her. "I'm not afraid of anything, anymore."

After the wake, my father and I went back to the small room we were renting. It had a bunk bed in, and although I had the top bunk, I let my father take it that night. I slept close to the floor, with a knife I'd stolen from Livia's house gripped in my hand under the pillow. They may have killed my mother, but they weren't going to get to my father. I'd protect him, no matter what.

I remember how I'd held the knife the whole night through, stayed awake whilst he slept, and in the morning when he'd woken, I told him I was ill and slept the day away. Everything looked better in daylight. My father would be okay. And he was, for a while.

*

In the woods, by the train station, the torch beam picked up a colour that shouldn't be there. A blue, which was unlikely to be just a patch of flowers.

"What is that?" Akono asked.

"Could be anything."

"Could it be your fiancée?"

"She isn't my fiancée."

"I think you're focusing on the wrong thing."

Freya wore blue quite a lot, or, at least, I pictured her wearing blue. I, on the other hand, wore dark clothes, black mainly. I didn't want to stand out. It wasn't what I liked.

"Yes. It could be her," I told the ghost.

"Then go and take a look."

"Why don't you mind your own business," I told him.

"Because the Sikkilite is my business. Now, do it before I call the other ghosts over."

"What sort of ghost are you, exactly, Akono?"

There was a pause. "An impatient one," he replied.

I took some deep breaths and walked towards the blue colour. At one point, I thought I could make out an arm or a leg and my stomach turned. The torch was still on low, so I flicked it up to high. The arm or leg turned out to be a thick branch or piece of bark that had fallen some time ago, and the blue was just a carrier bag.

"It's not her," I told Akono.

"Then we'd better keep searching."

There was a scuffing sound behind us, like a foot on tarmac. I held my breath, turned the torch off and moved away from the plastic bag.

"Someone else is looking for her," I said.

"Or looking for you," Akono added. He could be right. Perhaps Berg, the taxi driver, had come back, concerned for either my welfare or his torch.

"Hello," came a man's voice from the edge of the wood. "It's Constable Jackson from the police. Show yourself."

That was it. That was the thing I was forgetting. Constable Jackson knew where the bag had been found. He could easily have guessed where I was going to go next.

"The police should be able to help," Akono said.

"Not this one. This one wants me dead."

"Why would he want you dead?"

"I don't know. Because he's one of them. One of the people from Songström."

"Songström?" Akono asked, his interest piqued. "What do you know of Songström?"

"It wants me. I think it may be where they'll take Freya."

"Songström is not a place you want anyone going. Pray you find her before she gets there."

"This is Constable Jackson. Come out with your hands up."

121

"You should see what he wants," Akono said. "He might be able to help. He might have found out some more information."

It was the last sentence that made the most sense to me. I was in a fragile state, had been since the conversation with Freya in the café, and it was entirely possible I'd got it wrong about Jackson.

I switched the light back on and made my way toward the car park. When I reached the fence, I lifted the beam. Constable Jackson was standing by one of the cars.

"Who is it?" he called.

"Sammel Ahlberg," I answered. "I've been looking for Freya. Do you remember?"

"Of course. I thought it might be you. Have you found anything?"

"Nothing yet."

"Would you like some help?"

It sounded like a genuine offer, and however useful Akono was, help from another physical person would be welcome.

"I'd love some."

"I've got some stuff in here that might help you." He hit the bonnet of the car.

"Okay, I'll be right out."

I pointed the beam at the floor and headed back towards the gap in the fence. Akono wasn't coming with me, I could tell. He waited in the woods, watching, but not moving.

I found the gap and squeezed through. One of the pieces of wire snagged on my jacket and I heard it rip. It didn't matter. I could always find new clothes. I unhooked myself and continued across the flat ground towards the car.

I flicked the torch back at the woods. There were people there. I knew Akono would be there, tall and broad and dark, but there were others, too. A shorter person, maybe a child, a woman, tall and slim with red hair, and a man who looked like Teddy from the flats. They were gone in an instant, but they had been there.

I reached the car Jackson had been standing by, but he was gone. I walked around it and looked under it. I looked at the place on the bonnet that he'd patted, and there was a smear of something black, maybe oil, there.

"Constable Jackson?" I called. "Are you here?"

He wasn't. The sound of the words in the night air told me I was alone. I looked inside the car. It was messy. Food wrappers and receipts on the dashboard. Plastic bottles from drinks tucked into the door shelves. Some loose change in the ashtray. And a charger, too, coming out from the cigarette lighter socket. It seemed strange, but I recognised the charger, and the state the lead was in. It reminded me of Freya.

I stood back and looked at the vehicle. I didn't recognise it. It wasn't the regular shape of cars, more like a small Four-by-Four, though if it was any smaller, I'm not sure anyone could have fitted in the front seat.

Was that Freya's charger in the car? Was Freya a real person? I felt my anger rise. I wanted to know the truth. I had spoken to Freya so she must be real. So, how much had I made up? How much am I capable of making up?

It was impossible to know. The only action I could take was to go with my gut instincts. I recognised the charger, so this car was important.

I walked around it once more. There was a slight dent in the front bumper, and knocks on the edges of the passenger door. The trunk opened upwards and had fingerprints in the small layer of dust which clung to the paintwork. I pointed the torch at the fingerprints. They could have been Freya's. Could have been.

How did I not know about the car? The obvious answer was it was someone else's. But whose? I could feel my brain start to twist downwards, the thoughts multiplying, threatening to drag me to torturous depths. I kicked the wheel. I kicked the car. I shouted. I screamed. I let the redness take over. It was a release. A blissful release of rage that had been in me since the moment Freya had failed to return home. When had that been? It didn't matter. In my rage I didn't care. All I cared about was hurting this car that I knew nothing about.

*

When I was finished, and my rage abated, I sat down by the front of the car, exhausted. It left me no nearer the truth of her disappearance, but it felt better. I opened my bag, took out a bottle of water and drank a third of it, then rooted around for the container with the other cereal bar, and ate that.

I checked my phone; the clock read four minutes past midnight. There were no new messages, and the battery was under ten per cent. I turned it off, and put it in my jacket pocket. I dropped the container back into my bag, heard it hit my keys, and thought of something that made sense.

If this was Freya's car, or at least a car she knew, then she might have had the keys, and I'd found some keys inside her handbag, which had been abandoned near the station.

It was hard to breathe for a moment. I had put my thoughts together and they had made sense. More than made sense, they had worked something out. This was what it was like for everyone else. This was how it must be to be normal.

I unzipped the pocket on the sleeve of my jacket, and retrieved the three keys on the keyring with half a heart dangling on it. The heart made me angry again, but I fought against it. I'd had my five minutes of letting off steam. Besides, these might not be her keys at all. They could be someone else's that she simply offered to carry in a moment of kindness.

I looked at them under the torchlight, and was pleased to see that one of them could be a car key; most likely was. I stood, turned and inserted it into the door. It occurred to me, just before I twisted the key, the car might be alarmed, and I'd be setting it off by opening the door. It occurred to me, but I did it anyway. In truth, I would welcome the noise.

I rotated the key clockwise, and heard the central locking mechanism whirr.

So far, so good. I put my hand under the handle and pulled up. The door opened. No sound. No alarm. The light came on in the car, and it felt better. I switched the torch off, and looked in. The car smelt of Freya, of her perfume. I loved the smell, and it proved she'd been in the car at some point, probably recently.

I checked down the back of the driver's seat, and under the driver's chair; there was nothing but fluff and an empty sandwich packet. The sandwiches had been bacon and egg. Freya was a vegetarian, so they weren't hers.

I pulled myself up and into the seat, closing the door beside me. I pressed a few switches until at last I found the headlights. An arc of car park lit up before me. Next, I opened the glove compartment. If there was anything to be found, that could be the place to find it. My instincts were right; there were files crammed into the space. I lifted them out, and had a look at the sheets inside. They weren't Freya's. These were someone else's files: a woman named Vera.

It was a lead, as they said in the detective shows. This was Vera's car. Vera had taken her, or helped her disappear. She was complicit in Freya's disappearance. I would find her and she would tell me what had happened.

I shut the door of the car, and reclined the seat back. I needed some rest, and if this was Vera's car, there was a chance she'd return here, sooner or later.

I turned the headlights off, closed my eyes, and fell straight to sleep.

*

In my dream, I was in the car park, in the car. Something made a sound outside and I opened my eyes. Towards the corner, towards the place I'd seen the communications tower, a semi-circle of people were on their knees, arms held out in front of them, touching the ground. They were dressed in grey tunics, chanting in low voices. I attempted to turn the headlights on, but they didn't work.

I opened the car door, and stepped out. I heard my feet as they connected with the ground; a definite click, click. The low mumbling I had taken to be the people chanting, was in fact an electrical hum coming from the tower itself. It charged the night air with violent power.

I didn't walk directly towards the people. They frightened me. Instead, I chose to keep nearer to the fence, keeping my eyes on them all the way. They must have heard me, and heard my walking, yet none of them moved. Perhaps they were dead. I don't know why I thought it, but it was definitely a possibility.

"Hey!" I called, when I was as close to them as I wanted to be. "What are you doing?" They remained still. The thrum of the tower was far louder here, and it was possible they couldn't hear me over it.

"Hello!" I shouted at the top of my voice. The thrumming ceased immediately, and my telephone rang in my pocket. I took it out and looked at the screen. It just read 'Incoming call'. I'd never seen it say that before.

I pressed the green button at the bottom, and held it to my ear.

"Hello?"

"Hello, Sammel."

It was Freya's voice. Freya's voice coming out of the dark, coming out of the telephone.

"I'm looking for you, Freya. I'm staying strong and I'm looking for you."

"I knew you would."

"I'm trying to find Songström. Is that the right thing to do? Is Songström where you are?"

"Songström is as good a place as any."

"I found the car, the car at the station. I found Vera's car."

"Do you remember Vera?"

I thought about it, concentrated on the name till I could see little pinpricks of colour behind my eyes. No memory of her emerged.

"I can't, Freya."

"That's all right, Sammel. You mustn't worry. Worrying makes it worse. What you need to know is that Vera is a friend. You mustn't hurt her."

"I wouldn't hurt her. I wouldn't hurt anyone, Freya. You know that. Don't you? Don't you know that?"

"I do."

"I would never hurt you, never mean to hurt you. If I have hurt you in any way, I didn't mean to."

"You haven't hurt me."

"I can't remember Vera."

"You will. You just have to think about it. Think about it and you'll remember."

"How long have I got left? How long have I got left to save you?"

"A few more days. But you'll do it. Do you believe you will?"

"I'll try."

"You will, Sammel. You will save me, and I will save you."

The call was ended, and the people on the floor all stood as one. They turned and looked at me. They had no emotions on their face, and that was okay. I went back to the car, and got inside. I closed my eyes, because that was how I knew I would wake up, and, before I knew it, I was dreaming no more.

I could drive, I just couldn't legally drive. I put the car key in the ignition and twisted it. The engine turned over three, four, five times and then it started. It wasn't the prettiest sound, but at least it seemed steady.

I put my seat belt on, took the handbrake off, and pulled away, testing the clutch, making sure I had the feel of it, before venturing onto the road. It seemed manageable.

I couldn't think who Vera was, or, more importantly, where she lived, but it was likely to be in the town. I put the indicator on, twisted the steering wheel to the left, and went as fast as I felt happy going.

*

My father taught me how to drive when I was fourteen.

He didn't see demons, or, if he did, never admitted to it. He thought both my mother and I were victims of a chemical imbalance in our brains that caused us to hallucinate, and the doctors agreed with him. At least, they did about my mother; he never let them near me.

We moved again after my mother's funeral. Moved further out into the country, into a place he acted as a house-sitter for. It was a bit run down, but perfectly fine. The owner had been having problems with people using it illegally, so wanted us to live there to deter any vagrants who might come sniffing around.

130

The house suited us. It didn't have a name, which surprised me. I expected everything to have a name. Numbers were fine, but associating a number with a thing like a house I found difficult.

The house was very large, and my father had to walk around it twice a day, fixing anything that had gone wrong. He always asked if I wanted to go with him, but I rarely did. I stayed in the lounge and closed the doors. I was happier when I could see the doors were shut.

For the first few weeks we slept in the same room, my father having the single bed whilst I slept in the double. I told him I didn't need to, but he said he felt more comfortable in the single bed, as he woke each morning with no expectations. I wasn't sure what he meant, though thought it might have something to do with my mother. Everything back then had to do with her in some part.

We'd wake up at six. He'd shower first, and then I would. We'd be dressed and eating breakfast by six forty-five. Then we'd turn the house alarm off and he'd start to go through the rooms. It didn't take him long once he'd got used to it. By eight o'clock he was finished. If it was sunny we would go outside and kick a football around. I wasn't much good, but it didn't matter.

If it was raining we would do a puzzle, or my father would tell me stories about my mother until he got too upset to carry on. I didn't know whether this was a good thing or not. Whenever he cried, I would sit and hold his hand until he felt well enough to carry on.

131

Lunch would be either pizza, or chicken and vegetables. We had them on alternate days, and whilst he thought I liked the pizza best, I really didn't mind. In the afternoons, we studied. He said that was the time the brain worked best. We would find a book in the house library, and we would read a passage from it. Then we'd read it again and my father would talk around the things we read about, relating them to his own experiences. It may not have prepared me for any exams, but I did learn a lot, and listening to his voice and watching his face settled me.

His second run through of the house was at six in the evening, before any of the good television started. It would take half-an-hour, and he always made sure he'd shut and locked every internal door that could be locked. He'd check the external windows too, and only when he was completely happy would he set the alarm once again.

My father liked watching crime shows. They weren't my favourite, but they were all right. What I liked best about them were the theories he'd come up with about who'd done what, to whom, and why. He'd get it right, too, most of the time.

We'd go to bed at nine o'clock, and then sleep through to the next day. It was like this for almost a year. Peaceful, tranquil; we were getting on with life.

*

The first demon arrived a week before my birthday. I didn't recognise it immediately, because it took the form of a dog. Up to that point, they'd been people-shaped, but this one was a largish brown cross-breed. One day it wasn't there, and the next it was lying on the back lawn when I opened the door to put the rubbish bags out. It had immediately looked at me and wagged its tail.

I'd have called to my father, but he was having his post-lunch nap. He'd taken to having them, just recently, and would be crotchety if I woke him without good reason. Carefully, I pulled the door closed behind me, and walked as quietly as possible onto the grass. The dog stretched and stood as I approached, mouth open and wanting attention. I patted its smooth coat, and tickled under its chin. It had no collar, but it sat when I told it to.

I found one of the older footballs, and kicked it. The dog chased the ball, picked it up and brought it back. I patted its head again and it understood. We spent thirty minutes playing this game before it brought it back one last time, turned and trotted off into the forest that ran along the back of the property.

When my father woke, I told him about the dog, and he said it was cool, but to be careful, because any animal can turn nasty at any point, no matter how nice it initially appears to be. I nodded, but didn't believe it. I told him it didn't have a collar, and asked him if I could name it. He grinned, and we went into the library to find a good name from one of the books. After a few hours of searching, we came up with Moby. It was a name from one of my father's favourite stories.

Moby came by the next day. I'd asked my father if he wanted to meet it, but he said it was okay, the dog was my friend. In the morning, he'd searched through our belongings stored in the garage, and found me a tennis racquet and balls. I told him I'd never seen him play tennis, and he explained that the racquet had been his father's.

"It's only wooden," he said. "So, make sure Moby doesn't mistake it for a stick. It's very important to me."

"I won't," I told him. "I'll just use it to hit the balls."

The racquet must have made a difference, because Moby stayed a little longer that day. It liked chasing after the tennis balls, and it made me feel like I had a friend.

Moby began to visit every day, and after a week of chasing balls, we went on our first trip around the grounds. The dog was very interested in everything we saw, like it was seeing the world for the first time. It liked chasing birds, too, though Moby always held back a little, as if it didn't want to catch them. The dog especially liked the small pond with the statue of a girl that was also a fountain, splashing as much as it could in the water.

That was the day the second demon appeared. This one was person-shaped, standing at the edge of the forest when we returned from our tour.

My father was inside the house, but I didn't call for him; I didn't want to scare him. Besides, Moby was a friendly demon, so why shouldn't this one be?

The dog came and sat by my legs, and we both looked at the human-shaped demon, until, in the end, it disappeared. I didn't see it leave, but when I opened my eyes it had gone.

*

The next morning, the demon reappeared, in exactly the same spot. I watched it through the back door.

"Something out there?" my dad asked.

I nodded. "There's a demon at the edge of the forest."

"A demon? Is it coming any closer?"

I shook my head. "Just watching."

"Stay close to me, Sammel. Chances are it'll move on by nightfall."

He was right. That afternoon, when he'd fallen asleep, I returned to the back door. The figure had gone and Moby was waiting on the lawn. I thought about this for a moment, then opened the door and went out.

*

It all started as normal. We kicked the football a few times, and Moby brought it back. Then the dog returned it just slightly out of reach, which meant it wanted to play with the tennis ball.

I picked the racquet and ball up, and hit it a few times in different directions so Moby could fetch it. When I turned to hit it towards the wood the figure was there, watching again. It caught me by surprise, and I stepped backwards. Moby saw this, looked in the direction of the wood, and started to growl, deep in its throat. It didn't like this demon, and it was protecting me.

The hooded figure in the wood took a step closer. It was taller than any person I'd ever seen, and in no rush to reach us. It was clothed in off-white, loose robes, and afraid of nothing, including Moby. It took another step closer. I took another one back. Moby stood his ground and bared more teeth.

Another step closer, though step wasn't the right word for its movement. It glided.

"Stop where you are," I said to it. "Stop."

It didn't care. It was now at the edge of the lawn. I'd have retreated further if Moby hadn't stayed where he was. I didn't want it to hurt Moby, and in a way, we were protecting each other.

The figure glided closer again. Moby took a step towards it. I looked at the dog, wanted to call it back, but knew I shouldn't distract it. I took a step forward, too. The tall demon didn't move. It just waited, looking at me with its hidden eyes.

It raised its right arm, and there was a snapping sound within the mesh of trees behind it. A second or two later, a long branch came out and the demon caught it. Moby growled more.

The demon raised the stick above its head. Moby's growl momentarily grew louder, and then it changed, became deeper, so deep it no longer sounded like a simple dog. I looked at him, and watched, in awe, as he changed.

Moby's shoulders became bunched, larger, muscles appearing upon muscles. Its lean body elongated by several inches, and the turf underneath its feet was churned by its violent claws. Halfway down its body, something squirmed beneath its skin, until eventually, gruesomely, it burst through, and another powerful leg emerged. Moby was now twice the size, and the robed figure watched as quietly as I did.

The dog demon took a step closer, and screamed. It wasn't a bark or a growl, but then why should it be? Moby was not a dog. This creature, the creature it had become to protect me, was a corruption, and it screamed.

Something happened to the tall demon's cape. It started to thin, to shred, revealing the figure underneath. I had imagined it to be a skeleton, but logically, skeletons can't stand up. Of course, logically, dogs weren't demons who could grow more legs and scream, but at least Moby was following the real world to a fashion. It still had muscles, and I'm sure there's plenty of animals who can change shape, even slightly. Moby was just an extreme.

Moby's scream continued, loud and piercing, and I was pleased the dog demon wasn't directing it at me.

Finally, the cape fell away completely, revealing a face I knew; Livia's mother. She had found me here, and had been about to... do what? I didn't know. I didn't want to know.

Moby stopped screaming, and waited, panting hard from the effort. Livia's mother looked at me.

"I see you've got yourself a guardian," she said. "How sweet."

"Why are you here?"

"Livia told me you saw her arm had healed, and it's better to be safe than sorry. That's what I always tell them."

"Tell who?"

"It doesn't matter who, Sammel Ahlberg. What matters is we cover our tracks. Dispose of the people who can expose us. That's you, Sammel. You and your mother."

"You've already killed her," I said. Moby growled a little.

Livia's mother shook her head slightly.

"No, she killed herself, as well you know."

"You made her, you got inside her head and you made her!" I shouted.

"Did I? Am I here at all, Sammel? Do you see me, or do you simply want to see me?"

It was strange, but that was the first moment I noticed she wasn't wearing any clothes. I concentrated on her face.

"You are there. I know. What were you going to do to me?"

138

"I was going to make you disappear. Make you another missing person, never to be found."

"But you can't, Moby's stopping you."

"Oh, have you given it a name? How amusing." Livia's mother's voice was calm, in control, and it scared me a little. She smiled and held her arms out. "Do you see the countryside around here, Sammel Ahlberg? Do you think it's beautiful?"

She looked at me, but she wasn't waiting for an answer.

"Under the earth, stretching out for acres in every direction, hundreds of people are buried. I know about these people. We all do. We know they're here. We helped put them here. Some of them, Sammel, were buried alive; held down whilst the earth was shovelled on their heads, their shouts cut short by the dirt that filled their throats. You can't see them, but I can. I relive their fear like it was still happening. It's something beautiful, the world I see. Do you want to see them?"

Again, this was no question. Again, I offered no answer. Livia's mother raised her arms. Around us black outlines emerged through the ground and waited.

"This is all that is left, after the ghosts have leeched their emotions. They are useless, and I pity them. Making people afraid is a good thing, Sammel. It's a form of faith, and we know how powerful faith can be, don't we?"

She seemed proud of her words, like she'd been holding them in for a long time, waiting for the opportune moment.

"This house you live in," she continued. "Why do you think it's empty?"

This time she waited.

"I don't know," I said.

She laughed, mockingly. My words had somehow given her power.

"Because no-one wants to be here, Sammel, amongst these… shadow people. The world is full of sorrow, full to the brim and overflowing. And do you know what happens to that sorrow? Do you know where it goes? Inwards, because it hasn't anywhere else *to* go. Like a black hole sucking everything in, the sorrow builds, takes shape, warps the world around it. And, sooner or later, the world's going to buckle, and everything's going to get in, do you hear? Then people like you will be torn apart, Sammel Ahlberg. And who's going to be the first in line? I am. And I'm going to hurt you so bad you're not going to know where you are; heaven, hell or somewhere in-between. Do you believe me, Sammel?"

I didn't answer.

"Say something!" Livia's mother screamed. In that scream, I thought I noticed a transparency that wasn't there before. I thought I saw the trees and leaves behind her, through her. "Don't play dumb with me, boy. You're clever, aren't you? Trying to take her away from me. But I saw it. Saw it in her eyes. In the way she spoke.

140

I don't know why she liked you. She used to like me. Then I was second-best. I don't deserve second fucking best, Sammel Ahlberg. You interested her. You! A worthless piece of shit. She's different now. Different from the girl I knew, the girl I made."

Livia's mother was seething. I could feel a heat coming from her.

"I'm not going to be second-best," she spat. "I'm not going to lose her. Do you understand?"

I said nothing and watched as Livia's mother raged. It felt good.

"Why don't you answer me?" she shouted. "What sort of scum are you?"

I took a step towards her. In my hand, gripped tightly, was the tennis racquet. As Livia's mother had been talking, the racquet had been growing warmer. It felt like it had become part of my hand, my wrist. I walked forward with strength, and Livia's mother couldn't go anywhere. She was stuck, and I brought the racquet up and I hit her, across the face. I hit her arms so hard I broke them. I shattered her kneecaps, broke every rib in her body, and then finally, when she was on the floor, I brought the racquet down on her head, until there was nothing left but a mush of flesh and splintered bone.

I stepped back and watched. Whatever Livia's mother had been, started to become translucent. The blood that flowed from her body turned to ashes on the ground, and her bones glowed red with heat. When it had cooled a little, Moby came along and ate the jelly-like substance she had become, got its fill and slowly turned back into the dog it pretended to be.

When Moby had finished, I looked up and saw we were in the forest. I didn't remember going there. I didn't remember taking my clothes off, yet all I had on was my underwear. In front of me, ashes smouldered, and it was hard to see exactly what had been set alight, but it didn't matter. The sky was darkening, and I needed to go home.

*

Such was my apparent frequency in returning home without clothes on, the first question my father asked when I arrived back, was where the tennis racquet had gone.

"I left it in the woods."

"Well, I need you to go and get it. After you've got some clothes on."

I was worried. I couldn't remember holding the racquet after the attack on Livia's mother. It was likely to be smashed, or burnt, or covered in blood.

I took as much time as possible to find something to wear, and eventually my father appeared and put the clothes on me himself. Then he walked me to the back door and pushed me out.

"I mean it," he said, grimly. "You need to get me that tennis racquet."

"It's getting dark," I said to him.

"You should have thought of that," he replied. He got the torch off the windowsill. "Here," he said. "Don't lose this."

As it turned out, I needn't have worried. Moby was sitting at the edge of the woods, where Livia's mother had first appeared, the tennis racquet held delicately in its mouth. The dog dropped it when I came closer, and I patted its head.

There wasn't a mark on it.

"Thank you," I told Moby. The demon lay down and closed his eyes.

*

No new demons visited for a while. Moby's visits became irregular, until, one day, they finally stopped altogether. I thought it might be the end of the demons, that perhaps they had had their fill of me; that they wouldn't bother me anymore. I was older, after all. I thought, with age, everything might get easier. It wasn't true.

The demons had just found a different way to torture me.

*

In the coming weeks, my father began to lose energy. He wasn't able to play football for as long, and his naps grew longer. He smiled less and he sighed more.

One Tuesday morning, after checking the house, we got into the car and we drove to the nearest town to visit the doctor there.

I waited in the room outside, whilst my father was spoken to. The receptionist behind the desk looked at me, by turns caring and cold, and I couldn't decide whether or not she was a demon. If the business with Livia's mother had taught me anything, it was that anyone could be the enemy.

My father emerged with a long face.

"We're going to have to come back on Friday, Sammel," he told me.

"That's all right," I replied. "I don't mind."

We didn't go back to the same place on the Friday, instead driving further into the city. This time we visited a hospital, which, at least, had a better selection of toys, not that I played with them.

There were definitely demons in the hospital. I think it was the shadows that gave them away. Sharp pointed shadows where none should be. They reached out from corners to try and touch me. I kept moving, trying to keep my legs out of their reach. I could tell I was annoying people.

When my father reappeared, he looked worse than ever. Something was very wrong.

Two days later, he told me we were moving out of the house, and were going to stay with some distant family that lived in the city. I didn't say anything, and when he offered his arms for a hug, I held him as tightly as I could.

*

We had a week before we left the house, and it was in that week that he taught me to drive. He said it was important. He said it was a life skill he'd always wanted to teach me, and now was as good a time as any. I enjoyed that time. My father taught me so very much.

The day we left, I saw Moby one more time. At the edge of the woods, camouflaged by the trees. I pointed it out to my father whilst we stood at the back door, and, just for a moment, I think he saw it too.

*

I pulled Vera's car over into a bus stop. The town started quickly. One moment, I'd been flanked by trees and shrubs, the next, the road was lined with houses. Sitting in the car, I could feel the people moving within, could feel the crawl of them, like ants over my skin.

Where was Vera? Did she live in one of these houses? Freya said I knew where she lived, but I didn't. I couldn't know where everyone lived. I retrieved my phone, turned it on and opened the browser to access the internet. I looked down at the charger in the car and cursed the fact that I hadn't been charging the phone as I'd driven back from the station. It was a mistake. I hated making mistakes.

I plugged it in and the lightning symbol appeared over the battery. I typed in the site I used to look up people's addresses, and entered what I knew of Vera. It came back with a single result. Another couple of taps on the screen, and I was looking at the route to her house. Five minutes it said. Five minutes would be fine.

The petrol indicator was glowing red. That was all right. I still had money, and there was an all-night petrol station further along the road. That made me feel happier. One thing to fix another.

*

I pulled into the garage not knowing what side the cap was on. On the forecourt, a woman was holding two cones, as if she was about to close. I wound down the window.

"Are you open?"

"Yes," the woman replied. She looked sad. "We just had a delivery, I was opening back up again. Got lost in thought for a moment. Do you ever do that?"

"I do," I told her.

I pulled up to the pumps nearest the kiosk. It wasn't a large garage, not like one of the big chains you usually get. I sat and waited for the woman to go back behind her counter before I got out. I didn't want to talk to her anymore than I had to.

When she was settled, and drinking her mug of tea, I got out, closed the door, and inspected the side of the car. I couldn't see the cap on the driver's side. That was fine. At least it looked like I'd got it right. I walked around the back of the car, and saw it on the other side.

It had been a while since I'd operated one of these pumps but they were easy enough. I put in what I thought might be half a tank, and replaced the nozzle.

The kiosk was open, which was a surprise. A lot of garages would only have a small window to communicate through at this late hour.

I pushed open the heavy door and heard the buzzer sound. The woman looked up at me from behind the counter, pale, and frightened.

"Is everything okay?" I asked. She glanced out of the window.

"Can you see it?"

I turned and looked at where she was indicating.

"Do you mean the figure wrapped in sackcloth sitting on the petrol pump?"

She gasped, and her eyes grew wide. "You mean you can? You really can?"

"Yes."

"It's been there all evening and no one else can see it. I don't understand what it is."

"It's a demon," I said to her. "But it could be a good demon. Has it said anything to you?"

"No, it just looks. I don't like it."

"Is it the first demon you've seen?" The woman nodded. "Has something bad happened to you?"

This made her turn to look at me. "Why do you ask that?" she said, nervously.

"Demons are everywhere, but the fact that you can see this one means it may be drawn to you. They go where sadness is."

The woman paused, raised her fingers to her lips. Tears welled in her eyes.

"Oh, God," she said. "Oh, God, I thought I was past it."

I waited, watching the demon. Seeing what it did. It seemed to be looking at her.

"It might help if you tell me what happened," I said. "Please."

"I don't know you."

"Strangers are just friends who don't know each other," I said. "At least, that's what my father said once."

The woman looked at me, at the demon and then back at me.

"All right," she said, bringing a shaking hand up to her mouth. She was holding a tissue, and she used it to wipe her nose. "Eighteen months ago, my husband and I were arguing. I was walking Alex to school, he was five, and he, and he..." More tears fell. Faster, heavier.

"What happened to Alex?" I asked. It was important she told me everything.

"He... he got away from me, slipped my hand. I was arguing with my husband on the phone. I wasn't concentrating. I didn't realise he'd gone. I watched the truck go by. Oh, God, I watched the truck go by, and then I heard the screams. Three screams, I counted them. And do you know what? Do you know the worst thing? I don't know if any of those screams were Alex's. The truck hit him, and I wasn't there." A shudder ran through her body. "I wasn't there."

"What happened to Alex?"

"He died. At the scene. And that was it. That was the end of everything."

I waited a few seconds, maybe ten, then I said, in the softest voice I could. "Come with me. Let's face this thing together."

"Why? Why would you do that?"

"Because I see demons everywhere. And I think I can help you."

I stood back a little. The woman, who had a, 'Hi, I'm Connie!' badge pinned to her blouse, looked lost and confused.

"Can it harm me?" Connie asked.

"No more than you're harming yourself."

She put her mug down, straightened a non-existent apron, and stood up. "You've dealt with these things before?"

"Yes. Yes, I have."

"All right," she said, and walked to the end of the counter, one hand brushing along the top of its surface as if she thought she might collapse at any moment. "This is like a dream," she whispered, before rounding the end and emerging onto the shop floor. She crossed the cold linoleum, walking ahead of me. At the door, she stopped. "I'm nervous," she said.

"Good," I replied, stepping ahead of her, and opening the door. "There's nothing wrong with that."

*

We walked together to the pump and stood in front of it. The sackcloth moved gently in the wind.

"Who are you?" Connie asked.

"I am a messenger," the demon said.

Connie looked at me. The strangeness of the situation was dawning on her. Tears formed in her eyes. I nodded for her to continue.

"Who sent you?"

"You know who sent me."

Connie backed towards the station.

The demon turned. "I cannot leave until you listen..." it said. "I cannot leave until you listen. I have his car."

Connie stopped at that. Stopped as still as a statue. She stared at it with fierce eyes. "You have what?"

"His car. I have his car," the sackcloth demon stated.

"They never found his car. Are you telling me you took it?"

"No. I found it, so you might listen. That's all."

Connie was growing angry. It seemed to me she was getting larger, that her emotion was changing her. "Give it back! You give it back! I just want him back!"

"I cannot give him back."

Then, as quickly as she'd grown, she shrunk. Collapsed in on herself. Her knees sagged. Her back hunched over. She held out one weak arm.

"Then the car," Connie asked. "Please give it back. He used to kiss it every night. Twirl it in his hands. He said it was his lucky charm. He said... it kept us all safe."

"I am the messenger."

"You are a demon," I said to it. "That is what you are."

"Oh, and Sammel speaks. I thought the dog had got your tongue."

"You know me?"

"Sammel Ahlberg. Is there another who creates such sadness? You are our hero."

Connie stepped forward. "What is your message?" she asked.

"Very well. It is this. He went. Took three steps and was gone. It was not your fault."

"It was. I was there. Distracted. Stupid. I left him and... I saw the truck."

"It was an accident."

"My son was crushed, and I let him go."

The demon held up its hand and dropped something dark. It struck the floor with a click, and spun to a standstill. For a moment, I thought it might be Sikkilite, but when it stopped, I saw it was a pebble with concentric circles engraved on it.

"See?" the demon asked. It dropped another pebble. "See?" And a third. "See? That is all the time it took, and it is no time. You could not stop the stone from falling. You could not stop the truck from moving."

"But..."

"Three blinks and he was lost. You must move on or you will be lost too."

Connie looked stunned, like she might not be able to say anything else again. She dipped her head. "I am lost already," she said faintly. "Lost in a world of toys, pens and fifty-page puzzle books. Do you know..." she said, her voice rising, "... do you know I've picked a hole in the sheet where he used to lie?"

The demon nodded under its sackcloth. "I know. But this hole you will stitch. Sew it well and it will be safe. Take what he gave you. Let it shape your life and move you forward with new impressions."

"I can't. I can't move on. I'm not worthy of moving on."

"He wants you to move on. He held a flower for you and you took it; that's how you must remember."

"How... how can you know that?" Connie asked.

I watched Connie as she looked back up, towards the place the messenger had been. It was no longer there. "Don't go. Come back! Please..."

There was another click on the floor. I looked down and saw a toy fire engine, small. The size that a young child would play with. Connie saw it, staggered forward, and like the people around the communications tower, fell to her knees. She looked at the fire engine for a while, both in awe and in fear.

"I've not seen it in so long," she said. She moved her hands toward it, as if she was cradling the air around it. "Can I pick it up?"

"Yes," I said. "It's yours."

Carefully, delicately, Connie reached out and picked up the fire engine.

"Oh my," she said. "Oh, my."

I watched for a moment, and then moved to pick up the traffic cones. I walked them to the entrance and the exit and put them across both. I took some money out of my pocket and placed it under the bucket of sand near where Connie lay on the floor. She mumbled something. I couldn't quite make it out, but I like to think she said, "Thank you."

I got back in the car, and drove off. The demon had known my name, and said I was the cause of much suffering, the most suffering, and I didn't know what it meant.

*

I drove slowly, following the map on my phone to Vera's house, wondering how many others could see the demons. I'd not thought about it much, and had always assumed my mother and I were the only ones with the ability to perceive them.

Though, why should that be? It was likely that thousands of people could see them. Did that mean there were other people in the world on their own journeys? I tried to think about them, but my mind kept returning to the man on the beach. I thought he was me, but perhaps he was someone else. Perhaps he was on his own journey.

The woman, Connie, had said she hadn't seen them before. So, maybe they were getting stronger, breaking down the barriers, like Livia's mother had told me all that time ago.

What would that mean? Would Songström become the real world? Would the real world disappear? Was there anything I could do to stop it? Saving Freya was a personal mission. It wouldn't change Songström in any other way. Did I have to do something else now? Was saving Freya no longer important?

I stopped the car. I couldn't think about all these things and concentrate on what I was doing.

Was there somewhere else I'd seen Songström come through? At my flat, of course, and maybe at the train station with Akono. Where else had I been? There was the seafront, the bar with the girl who'd appeared in my dream. There was Garrick's mother, but he'd said she was okay. I waited for a feeling, something that would tell me what to do next. Sometimes I can sit for hours like this, and sometimes I know what I should do immediately.

A picture entered my head. A picture of the pier, stretching out over the blackness. Something was there, waiting for me. Perhaps it might have some answers, perhaps not. I'd go there, after I'd visited Vera's. I had to find out why her car had been at the station, first. I shifted into gear, lifted the clutch slowly, and joined the grey tarmacked road, with its all but non-existent traffic.

*

The further I travelled, the narrower the roads became. There was something deeply familiar about the route, as if, perhaps, I'd come this way before. I squinted my eyes and tried to picture the landscape as if it was daylight. I so very nearly had it. The way the sun reflected off the buildings. It was like turning the car engine over, and waiting for it to fire. I was waiting for my brain to fire, for the thought to spark and get everything going. It didn't happen. It was close, but being close wasn't good enough.

I parked outside the address I'd found for Vera, and looked up into her darkened windows. No one was in and there was a 'Sold' sign on the lawn outside. Had she moved on? It was possible. Was that why she'd left the car at the station?

I felt unwell. I felt like something was living inside me, in my gut. It squirmed, it expanded, it consumed. There are creatures that live inside people, but that wasn't what it was. I knew what it was.

Well, part of me did.

I wanted to get out and investigate, but this thing stopped me. It didn't want me to find out about Vera. I thought about taking the patch off my stomach, about using my hands to rip open the wound, and grab whatever it was. When I looked down, I'd already undone my jacket without realising.

"No," I said to myself, quietly.

I fastened my jacket back up. I'd have to come back. I'd have to come back and see what was inside Vera's place. Perhaps after the pier. Yes, that sounded sensible.

I'd wait till then.

*

The seafront was as deserted as the rest of the town. The lights were on along the promenade, so it felt a bit more welcoming, but not by much. I drove along towards the bar with the windows down, letting the air chase out any early morning cobwebs. After the seafront, I'd find a place to sleep. Maybe then breakfast, too. I was feeling hungry.

I pulled up and looked out at the pier. It was shut, but that didn't matter, I could wait here until it opened again. Turning the lights off, I leant the chair back, and rested.

"Where are you, Freya?" I asked aloud. There was nothing, no noise in return. I thought briefly about what she might be doing right now. What did people who were dead do? Ones who had Sikkilite, that is. It kept them safe, but what were they experiencing? I closed my eyes against the glare of the streetlights.

*

When I woke, it was two hours later. It was still dark, and the lampposts continued to blaze. Hardly anything had changed. I yawned deeply, got out of the car and stretched. Nothing felt strange, nothing indicated the presence of either a demon or Songström.

My hands were dirty, and for a moment my mind was blank. Then I remembered the search in the woods. The whole experience with Akono at the station felt like it had happened such a long time ago.

Should I be this muddy? It confused me. Things happened and I didn't understand. Things happened and... I heard the waves rolling in and knew what I had to do.

*

The beach used to make me feel anxious. It wasn't the vastness of it; that I could deal with. It was whatever lurked beneath, whatever threatened to tug at your legs, unseen. Fortunately, Freya hadn't been afraid. In fact, she'd have loved to be in it. It'd been her who'd cajoled me into entering it that very first time.

*

I reached the shoreline, and dipped my hands below the surface, rubbing them together. The trick, Freya had told me, was to understand that I was far more frightening than anything living under the water. When you are the danger, everyone else becomes the victim.

When I brought my hands back up, they were clean. I felt clean.

"You're not a bad man, Sammel," a man said behind me. "Sometimes we all do bad things."

I turned and saw Teddy, sitting on a groyne. His legs were crossed, and he was leaning forward.

"You know me?" I asked.

"We talk."

"What about?"

"About the place you never talk about."

"Songström? Is that where we are now?"

"We are where we are," Teddy said with kindness.

"When we talk about Songström, how does it end?"

"It ends when I tell you what Songström really is."

"What is it?"

Teddy stood up and kicked me in the head. I shouted.

"That is what it is, Sammel. It is pain. It is suffering. Songström is Hell."

I looked at Teddy and saw that he meant every word. I had never thought to call Songström anything other than its name. But it could be Hell.

"Does that make us dead?"

Teddy shook his head.

"Hell's not for the dead, Sammel. Hell's for the living, don't you feel that?"

I did. I felt that and I felt the throbbing where Teddy's boot had landed on my head.

"Can you tell me how to find Freya?"

"No. Freya is yours. Your secret."

"What secret?"

"You know it. It is the thing that presses the inside of your skull. It wants to be out, but you push it back constantly. You tell me you're worried your head might explode."

"I don't remember saying that. I don't remember speaking to you."

"Do you remember the phone call, Sammel?"

I shook my head, carefully. "What call?"

"Never mind. There's still time. I think there's still time."

"Are you a good man, Teddy?"

"I am not," he replied. "But I must deal with that myself. I am where I deserve to be. This is my Hell. When I'm ready, I will let it go. You must ask yourself when will you let yours go."

I shrugged. "I don't know. Perhaps after I've found Freya."

"Do you know how long you've been looking for her, Sammel?"

"A few days."

Teddy nodded, but there was sadness on his face. He stood, and I braced myself.

"What's the matter?" he asked. I looked at his boot and he laughed. "You still think I kicked you? Look at your hand."

I looked. I was holding a pebble, a pebble like the sackcloth demon had dropped at the garage. It had blood on it.

"I hit myself?" I asked, but I asked it of no one. Teddy had gone and I was on the pier.

The pier was a lonely place to be that morning. The waves and the seagulls were the only sounds to keep me company, and everything felt empty. I thought about leaving, but had nowhere else I really wanted to be, so I walked along the wooden slatted floor to the end, and stared out at the ocean. There were creatures in the water that wanted me to go and be with them. To climb over the railings and drop like a stone into the sea, the salt water covering my body, until I was nothing more than a piece of driftwood.

I spat, and watched the saliva fall to the surf.

"There," I said, "that's all of me you're having."

The metal legs of the pier creaked a reply. "We'll have you yet," they said.

"Perhaps."

*

I walked back along the pier, passing empty concessions. I tried to imagine what they might have been like in the past. Conversations, purchases, fights, laughter. It wasn't just a building above the sea; it was alive, and we were the parasites that lived on its back.

Along the seafront, a car's headlights moved in front of the tall houses. It wasn't travelling fast. It wasn't trying to get somewhere. It was searching. I wanted to believe it was searching for a lost pet, or a family member after a quarrel, but I knew it wasn't. It was looking for me.

I stood by the concessions, watching the car move along the road. The lights disappeared behind the pier entrance, and I held my breath. It should only take a few seconds to reappear. If it reappeared, I'd be safe.

Five seconds went by with no car. Nine seconds. Nothing. Twelve seconds, thirteen seconds. Nothing.

I heard a car door slam. They'd gotten out. They knew I was here. I had to hide. I went to move, but where I'd put my hand against the wooden wall of an old ice-cream kiosk, it was stuck.

I looked at where my hand should be, but now it was part of the wood. I could feel its bones still, could feel the individual fingers, but they weren't visible. I panicked, and pulled again, watching my wrist move. Footsteps started along the pier's wooden slats. They sounded like heels. I couldn't move and I couldn't escape.

"Okay," I whispered.

Instead of pulling, I pushed my hand further into the wood. It slid easily. I turned my body, so my back was against the concession, and I was facing out. I was afraid, not of the driver, but of disappearing forever into the wood, of not finding Freya.

When I was no longer separate from the building, I stopped. I blinked, but there was nothing to blink with. I went to breathe, but I had no throat, no lungs. I smiled. I felt happy.

The heels sounded louder now. They were confident. They knew I was on the pier. They thought I couldn't get off.

I could see everything in all directions. Everywhere the concession had a surface, I could use it to look out.

She walked past, but I couldn't see her properly. I should have been able to; the lights were working fine, but whenever I tried to focus on her, she disappeared.

Then I understood. She was in Songström, trying to break through.

The heels stopped and turned. She was confused. She knew I was here, but couldn't find me. I waited, watching as she flickered in and out of view. I got a glimpse of her face, but there was nothing there. Like the old woman in the hut, or Garrick's mother.

The woman paused. What was she doing? What was she thinking? The heels started again, heading back towards the pier entrance. I wondered how I was going to detach myself from the concession. Was I ever going to be a normal person again?

It was stupid. I'd lost focus. There was a scream, a thud, and I was back on the pier, near the entrance gates, standing over a woman lying on the ground.

"Hello?" I said, but I could tell she was unconscious.

I bent down and checked she was still breathing. She was. There was something familiar about her. I put her into the recovery position, and when I tilted her head, I recognised her instantly. She was the barmaid I had spoken to, who'd given me the envelope of photographs, who'd appeared to me in the dream. What was she doing here?

I felt guilt. I remembered her saying to come and find her, and I'd forgotten about it. She'd been in Songström, and now she was lying unconscious on the floor. It was linked. It was all linked.

I found my telephone and tried to call for an ambulance. Nothing happened. No ring tone, no pick up. It made no sense, it should have worked; emergency services should have worked.

I tried again. Still nothing. I looked around, along the promenade in either direction, searching for phone boxes. There were none.

"Shit," I whispered.

The car was close. I put my arms under the girl's shoulders and thighs, and lifted. She was lighter than she looked.

*

I carried her as fast as I could, being careful not to knock her against anything. When I drew level with the car, I propped her up, my shoulder in the crook of hers, and fumbled the car keys out of the front pocket of my trousers.

There was the smell of alcohol about her, but that didn't mean she'd been drinking. She worked in a bar, after all. There were days when I'd leave the supermarket, and I'd still be able to smell it on me even when I got home, and Freya would say... well, in truth, I don't know what she'd say.

I opened the passenger door, and manoeuvred the barmaid into the seat. I secured her restraint, and got into the driver's side.

Within seconds, we were on the road, heading for the hospital. I knew the way, remembered the scenery. That was good. That meant we were in the real world.

*

I carried the barmaid into the hospital, and they put her on a trolley and wheeled her away.

"Is she your girlfriend?" they asked me.

"Yes," I lied. I didn't want to leave her alone. I knew how quickly Songström could appear, and there would be things there that would want to keep her. If I said I was her boyfriend it meant I could remain close to her.

"What happened?" one of them asked me.

"I don't know. That's how I found her. I think she might have been drinking."

They got to a set of doors, and a nurse told me to wait there.

"Look after her," I said to them. "Please."

"We will," the nurse replied.

*

I waited. An hour rolled by, and then another. I piled the magazines so the bottom right-hand corners met. I arranged the chairs so they were in a circle. Once, I woke up standing at the window, which overlooked a courtyard of strange art.

"Hello," came a voice behind me. At first, I thought it might be Freya, but when I turned, it was only the nurse.

"How is she?" I asked.

"She's recovering. It looks like she had ingested a lot of alcohol and paracetamol. We pumped her stomach, and tried to counteract the drugs. She's okay for now. You were lucky you found her in time. A bit longer and... well, it wouldn't have been good. She owes you her life."

"When can I see her?"

"You can be with her now, if you like. Follow me."

"Thank you."

*

The hospital room was dim, dark grey and depressing. Vertical blinds hung over the window, and the lights on the instruments only seemed to highlight how grim everything was. I sat in a chair on the far side of her bed, whilst the nurse pointed out the button I needed to press if there were any problems. I thanked her, and she left.

The room was warm and quiet, and I felt safe. Hanging on the end of the bed was a clipboard with some of the girl's details on. I couldn't make out her surname, but her first name was Selina. I didn't know any Selinas.

Standing at the end of the bed, I watched her breathing. It seemed steady, and that made me happy. It briefly crossed my mind I

165

should be out looking for Freya, but something felt wrong, like I'd been approaching it in the wrong way. Over the past forty-eight hours I'd seen a great many things, but none of them had truly helped me. At least being with Selina might make some sort of a difference.

To my right was a door to an en-suite bathroom. I didn't know hospital rooms had such things. The room I'd woken in earlier certainly hadn't had one. It even had a shower. I looked at Selina once more, and decided it'd be fine if I used it while she slept. She wasn't going to know.

The shower was warm, and I was careful not to get my dressing too wet. There was soap, which I used to wash my hair, and it made me feel a lot better. Sometimes, water seems to wash away more than just dirt.

I dressed in the same clothes, and opened the bathroom door. The light in the room seemed a little darker, and Selina's breathing had changed; it was shallow, rasping. There was something else, too. A tube that hadn't been there before, attached to her collarbone, and snaking off towards the main door.

Songström was here.

I ran and grabbed the button the nurse had shown me and pressed it. Nothing happened. No buzz, no light. I pressed it again, several times; it wasn't working. I pulled at the cord connecting it to the wall and watched the wire come away, its end cut.

I stopped and listened. Under all this sudden horror, there was another sound I'd missed. A sucking noise. Rhythmic, unrelenting. I looked at the tube, saw it move with the sucking. I grabbed the torch out of my bag and shone it into the corner. Something was there. A dark shape into which the tube ran. There was no face, nothing I could recognise.

I grabbed the end of the tube attached to Selina's collarbone and yanked it. There was a moan, a deep moan, and the dark shape looked up. I yanked again, it wasn't going to have her. The sucking increased, doubling. I knew the monster couldn't hurt me, but it could kill her.

I pulled at the tube with everything I had, but it still didn't give. How could it be so firmly attached to Selina? I couldn't work it out, and didn't have the time to waste. I had to change tact. Holding the tube in one hand, I followed it down the side of the bed, to the rails that could be raised or lowered.

That was it. I placed the piping between the base and the handrail, and pushed it down until it was jammed, pinching it closed. Almost closed. I crouched on the ground and pulled on it with all my might, everything I had left to give.

The creature roared, and the sucking noise stopped. Then it began to cough, then to wheeze. I turned and saw it begin to spasm. Without the connection to Selina, it couldn't survive. I watched in awe as its structure collapsed like a water balloon splitting, its awful innards washing all over the floor. It was gone.

I pulled myself up using the handrail. Selina looked white. Dead white. I ran around the end of the bed, careful not to slip in the liquid, opened the door into the hospital and shouted for help.

They would never believe me. They would never believe there had been a monster in the room.

*

After they patched her up, they told me Selina had been losing blood from an internal bleed, which they'd managed to repair. They'd told me in my haste I had knocked over the water jug, which had spilt all over the floor. I'd also managed to sever the panic button when its cord got caught between the bed and the handrail. I listened as they told me all this. It fitted. Everything fitted, yet was different to what I'd seen.

They wheeled Selina away, and someone stayed with me until the orderly arrived to mop up the water. When all the liquid had been dealt with, I went back in and sat in the chair.

I couldn't work anything out. I had seen the monster burst and its innards cover the floor, but all it had been was water. And the tube the creature had been sucking on was just the cord for the buzzer. It made sense. It made no sense. I put my hand in my pocket, and retrieved the necklace, the Sikkilite.

Was it really Sikkilite? I knew it wasn't a real thing. I held my head in my hands and tried to keep myself from screaming. I needed to know what was real. I needed some sort of validation I wasn't going mad.

"Sammel," said a familiar voice.

"Akono? Are you real?"

"Better believe it," he said.

"Can you help me?"

"I've come to take you to her."

"To Freya?"

"To Freya."

"What about Selina?"

"Whilst you remain here, she is in danger."

"I saved her."

"You had to save her because she was near you. Songström will affect the ones you are closest to."

"Then where do we go?"

"Away."

"All right, Akono. All right. I'm ready."

"No, Sammel. I don't believe you are."

*

I wrote my phone number on a piece of paper and left it on the bed. Akono didn't like the idea and suggested I cut all ties there and

169

then, but I told him that wasn't the sort of person I was, or wanted to be.

I walked through hospital corridors, following signs to the exit. When, at last, I found it, I saw daylight streaming in. I had lost all track of time. A person, a young woman, weary and worried, travelled from the car park towards the hospital entrance. I stopped her, and asked her what day it was.

"Tuesday morning," she said. She looked at her phone. "Six-twenty AM." She smiled at me, and then the smile became broader. "How are you doing?" she asked.

"I'm surviving," I replied.

She patted me on the arm. "That's good. Take care," she said, and walked away.

*

"I only have a couple more days left," I said to Akono.

"It's plenty of time," he replied.

I walked on, past the car park, over the road, and into a green space beyond, where shaved lawns flanked me on either side. Ahead there was a building. A café by the look of it. Shut, of course, but there were seats around the front, and I lay down on one of them. The sky was clear, now. I could no more keep up with the weather, as I could with the time.

"Are you still here?"

"I am," Akono replied.

"I think I'm mad."

"And many would call you such."

"My father thought I was."

"Your father is a person, and a person can be wrong."

"My father is dead," I told Akono. He said nothing. "Akono?"

"I am still here."

"My father is dead, isn't he?"

"Did you ever see his body?"

"I was too young."

"You were sixteen. You were old enough."

"Are you suggesting he might still be alive?"

"I am just telling you that you cannot be certain. And I think you know I tell the truth."

*

The last time I saw my father, we visited a park. He looked pale and thin. Something was wrong, and I didn't know what it was.

We sat on a bench, much like the one I was lying on now, and we watched the people play on the grass before us.

He took my hand. "I'm going to go away," he said. "And you can't come with me."

"I'd like to come with you," I told him.

"I know," he replied, "But this is something I need to do on my own. I'm not well, Sammel. Not well at all, and it's only going to get

171

worse. I don't want to suffer, and I don't want you to suffer. Leaving is the best option for everyone."

"What am I going to do? Who am I going to live with?"

"You'll have the money, and it'll last a while. I've arranged for you to stay with someone, a great-aunt of mine, for as long as you need. She'll help you. And then, when you're ready, you can find your own way in the world."

"But I don't know her."

"Strangers are just friends you don't know yet."

"When... when... are you going?"

"This afternoon."

"But... what about... everything?"

"Everything changes. And we need to change with it."

I hugged him then. I cried and cried. I didn't want him to leave. I had no one else in the world.

Afterwards, when I felt better, I drove us to my great-aunt's house, where she made us tea and kept out of the way.

*

I remember it was sunny when the taxi came to take my father to the airport, and I remember thinking that was wrong. The whole thing was wrong.

"Let me come with you?" I asked him. "Just to the airport?"

He paused before answering, and for a few blissful moments I thought he was going to say yes.

172

"I'm afraid not, Sammel," he said. "This journey is just for me."

I screamed and I shouted. I lashed out and I hurt people. I couldn't cope, but I've never been able to cope. I thought it might never stop. I thought I might be lost and angry forever, but as the taxi pulled away, I quieted. Then it was real. Then I was alone. He turned and smiled a painful smile through the back window.

That afternoon, I stayed at the door in case he returned, in case he remembered his toothbrush, or his favourite shirt, or just that his son was waiting for him.

*

For the first two days, my great-aunt didn't say much. I spent a lot of time sitting in my new room, looking out of the window, down onto the road.

On the third day, she made a stew. I hadn't eaten since my father left, and the smell of it was enough to wake me from my lethargy. I went downstairs into the kitchen, and stood watching as she ladled it into bowls, and placed them on the table.

I found a spare chair, sat down, and we ate in silence. It tasted good, and when I'd finished, she picked up my bowl and gave me some more.

"Have you heard from my father?" I asked.

"He landed safely. I'm sorry for all that's happened, Sammel."

I shrugged. "It's not your fault."

*

There was a chance my great-aunt was still alive, and, if so, she'd probably know the truth of what happened to my father. I didn't know if she lived in the same house, but it was worth a try. It meant having to return to the old country, and to do that, I'd need to take a train to see her.

I lay on the bench with my eyes closed and the beginnings of this new plan, and that made me feel happy. I didn't sleep, just listened to the world as it began to wake up, and for once, it didn't involve demons or ghosts or Songström.

The world was just the world, and I lay within it.

*

I felt a tap on my shoulder, and I opened my eyes. Above me a figure stood, tall and broad.

"Are you having breakfast?" the figure asked. "If you're homeless, then I can make you a little something."

I pulled myself up into a sitting position, and smiled at the man. "I was only resting. But I would like breakfast, if you don't mind. I have money."

"Ha!" he said. "Money is better for the accounts. Come in when you're ready. Would you like the works?"

"That would be great."

*

The park was busier now. People made their way through it, to work or to the hospital or perhaps just to have a stroll in all the greenery. It was a pretty place.

I got out my phone, and switched it on. Three per cent charge. I waited for messages, but nothing came through. I was alone, again.

A party of parents passed by with their children, on their way to school. I wondered how they felt, the children. I wondered if any of them had ever visited Songström, that unholy and surreal place, and if they had, were they now, too, simply trying to live their lives in-between the bizarre and the demonic?

A bird fluttered down onto the table next to me. A black bird with twinkling eyes. It looked across at me, its head tilting first one way, and then the other. It was seeing if I had any food, if I was worth bothering with. I held out my palms, and it got the message. *No food here.* It flew away.

I heard the door swing open and I turned to see the man carrying a tray towards my table. On the tray was a cup and saucer.

"Here you go," he said. "Didn't know what you wanted, but thought coffee would be best this early in the morning."

He put it down in front of me, along with a holder full of sugar.

"Thank you," I told him.

He nodded his head and returned inside. I opened several of the sugar packets and added them to the cup. The first sip was the best. It made me feel warm inside.

I didn't know who I was. I sat there with the birds and the trees and the people and the grass, and I thought 'Who am I?'

"Hello," came a voice from in front of me.

I looked up. It was Bobby. It made me start, made me almost drop my cup.

"Bobby?"

"Didn't mean to surprise you."

"How can you be here?"

"You text me. You don't remember, do you?"

I shook my head.

"Fucking great, that is. Can I sit down?"

"Yes. Please."

I watched Bobby sit himself down on the chair opposite.

"Did you deal with the police okay?"

"The police?"

"At the flat? You went to deal with them."

"Yeah, wasn't a fucking problem."

"But..." I started, then fell silent. Bobby squinted at me.

"You all right?" he asked.

"No, Bobby, I'm not. I'm not all right at all."

"Well, welcome to the fucking party," he said, and laughed.

"No, I mean it. I think I'm hallucinating. Something's wrong. I can't tell what's real. I think I may have imagined everything."

"Lift up your shirt," Bobby said.

"What?"

"Lift up your shirt."

I did so, underneath was the gauze pad, held on by four pieces of long tape.

"You want to know if you imagined everything?" he asked. "You take that off. See if Garrick really stabbed you. If there's nothing underneath, you're a psycho, but if there is..."

I ripped it off in one quick movement. Bobby smiled. "There you go, need any more proof?"

"I guess not."

I pulled my shirt down.

Bobby leaned back in his chair. "Where you off to now?" he asked.

"I'm going home. Find out what happened to my father."

"Want some company?"

"Really? You'd come with me?"

"Better than that shit-hole supermarket, right? What time you leaving?"

I checked my phone. One percent left. "Three hours. At the station." Bobby looked at his watch.

"Meet you there. I've got a couple of errands to run first." He stood and walked away.

"Hey, Bobby," I called after him. He kept going. "Thanks."

He stopped, turned and looked at me. There was something in his eyes, something he nearly said aloud. In the end, he just shrugged, and walked away.

I heard the door open behind me. "Do you want some food?" the owner said.

"Yes, please."

*

He brought out two plates and set them down on my table. He was in his early sixties, with a healthy air about him.

"Now, eat up and thank me later."

I smiled, picked up the cutlery and began.

"Who are you?" he asked.

"I'm Sammel," I told him, through a mouthful of scrambled eggs.

"Have you been to the hospital?"

"Why do you say that?"

He pointed to the dressing that was now on the seat beside me.

"Oh, yeah."

The owner picked up his cutlery. "Have I seen you somewhere before?" he asked, as he began to cut his bacon.

"I don't know. I work at the supermarket, near the café. Do you know that one?"

He nodded. "I used to shop there. The supermarket, that is."

"Have you had the café long?"

"Not really."

I took another mouthful of scrambled eggs. It tasted different. It tasted disgusting.

"Do you like your breakfast?" he asked.

I could feel them now, feel them squirming against the inside of my mouth, against the inside of my cheeks. I stood, turned and spat out my food. White maggots sprayed everywhere. I retched, once, twice, and then everything came up.

I looked back at the owner. He had no face, no inside to his head at all, and yet he was laughing. Laughing hard. "Oh, something not right with it?" he asked through the laughter. "We'll have to get the owner."

I stepped back, over the seat, and onto the ground behind me. Still I could feel the maggots in my mouth, in my throat. I heaved again.

"She's dead, you know. Freya, she's dead."

I didn't reply, I didn't look at the thing. If the worst it could do was talk, then it was nothing to be afraid of.

"Do you know how she died? Do you want to know?"

I took another step away from it. Why did its face look like that? It must mean something, but I was in too much shock to think about what it might be.

"Let me tell you," the thing said.

"No!" I shouted automatically.

"Ah, there it is. That's it, isn't it? Don't you see?"

"There's nothing to see."

179

"Yes, there is. You don't want to know how Freya died. You're afraid to find out."

"I don't need you to tell me! She'll tell me. I want to hear it from her."

"Perhaps you don't need to," the thing with no face said. "Perhaps you already know."

I shook my head. "I don't."

I was further away now, by the side of the café.

"Let me tell you then, let me remind you how she died."

There came another voice then, inside my head. "Let me deal with it," Akono said.

"Please," I replied.

I closed my eyes to it all. Closed my eyes and let Akono do what he said.

*

When I opened them again, I was along the seafront, near the town, sitting on a bench and looking out across the water.

"Is it done?" I asked.

"It is done," Akono replied. "Time to move on."

I went to the shops and bought washing stuff, clothes, and a small case on wheels with a long handle that I could pull along behind me. It all fitted in there; everything I had, everything I was.

Then I went to the taxi rank, got in the front car, and asked them to drive me to the station.

180

I was on time. It didn't surprise me. I was always on time. Bobby was already there, waiting on the platform with two tickets in his hand.

"This the right place?" he asked, handing me one of the tickets.

"Perfect," I replied. "It's a sleeper train."

"Yeah, got us the same room. That okay?"

"Yeah, I could do with having you around. This place is crazy."

Bobby put a hand on my shoulder. "Crazy is what I do best."

There was a vending machine on the platform, and I bought a chocolate bar and a diet drink.

"That's one way of equalling everything out," he said.

The train arrived late. It wasn't the sleeper, but a connecting train. Bobby and I watched out the window as the scenery passed by.

We got off a while later, and had another hour to wait at the main station. There were cafés there, so we sat down by the window of one. I ordered a latte, and Bobby ordered two beers.

"No point in asking for one when I'm going to drink it straight down," he said.

"The owner of that café, he was a demon," I said to him.

"What *are* demons?" Bobby asked.

I thought about this. "They look like people, but say these terrible things. And they try to attack you."

"One of them ever hurt you?"

I thought back to Songström with the old woman who tried to pin me down. "No," I admitted. "None of them have ever hurt me."

"So, they're a type of person who says nasty things?"

"I suppose."

"Well, that just about sums up every fucking person I ever met. Including me. Have you heard what I say about some people?"

"I'm afraid I have," I told him. We both laughed.

The drinks came, and true to his word, the first beer disappeared in seconds. He belched, and relaxed.

"What do you think is wrong with me?" I asked Bobby.

"I really don't know. But I've thought about trying something. You want to give it a go?"

"Um, well. Is it dangerous?" I asked.

"Only one fucking way to find out."

"All right. Yes. Let's give it a go."

"I need you to tell me your happiest memory of you and Freya. The happiest moment you can remember."

"That's easy," I told him. "It's when we first met. It was lovely."

"Okay. What about the second happiest? Here." Bobby put his hand into his inside pocket and produced a biro. Then he found a folded-up piece of paper in another pocket and he put that in front of me. "Write it down. The second happiest memory from the past... how many years have you been together?"

"Two years."

"Must be a few memories to choose from."

"I guess."

Bobby sat back and sipped his second beer. He didn't look at me, instead concentrating on the patrons of the café. I sat there and tried to think back to the places Freya and I had been; the bars, the cinema, the holidays. I could remember the places, could remember a surprising amount of details, but the one thing I couldn't remember was Freya being there.

"Okay," Bobby said. "Write down the last conversation you had with her."

"I remember that," I said. "That was Friday lunchtime."

Bobby indicated I should start writing, so I did. I wrote about the Sikkilite, and putting it around her neck. About how tight the cord was. It took a few minutes, and in the end, I had to stop because there was no more paper to write on. I passed it over to him, and he read. Then he smiled. A sad smile.

He retrieved something from his back trouser pocket. It was the notepad he'd taken off the fridge in my flat. Bobby put it next to the piece of paper I'd just written on. He turned them to face me.

"You see it, right? You see what I'm getting at?"

I nodded. There was no doubt about it. They had the same handwriting.

"Freya didn't write the shopping lists at all. I wrote them, and I wrote them because she isn't real."

"No, no, no," Bobby said. "Freya's real, I'm certain. She's just not the person you think she is."

I took a moment to let his words sink in. Freya was not my girlfriend. I tried to think back over everything that had happened in the past few hours, to see how any of it made sense, but, of course, it didn't.

"Then who is she?" I asked. Bobby shrugged.

"How the fuck would I know?"

*

We drank the rest of the time away in silence, then caught the sleeper train, where I made full use of the shower. It was nine PM when I'd finished. I returned to the cabin, where I found a note from Bobby saying he was in the bar, if I needed him. I didn't. I got into the bottom bunk, and relaxed.

There was a power point in the cabin, and I plugged my phone in and waited for it to charge. I saw the bag that Constable Jackson had said was Freya's, and I wondered whose exactly it was. I looked in the purse again. There was nothing with a name. No ID. Just receipts, some money, and some café loyalty cards.

"I'm chasing a ghost," I said to the cabin.

I lay back on the bunk and sighed. Above me, the mattress moved.

"Who's there?" I asked.

"It's me," Freya replied.

"It can't be you," I told her. "You don't exist."

"Do you have the Sikkilite?" she asked me. I didn't respond. Why should I? Whatever was happening, was happening in my own head. There was no reason to continue the charade.

"Do you have the Sikkilite?" she asked again. "It's important."

"Yes," I said. "I have the necklace made of Onyx."

"It's made of Sikkilite. What the hell's gotten into you?"

"Apart from a couple of hundred maggots and some scary hallucinations?"

"It's what they do, Sammel. You know that. They make you doubt everything. They want you to feel like you're insane. The confusion gives them power."

"Well, then, they have the power."

"No, they don't." Freya said. "They don't have the Sikkilite."

I could feel myself losing my temper. I got the necklace from my pocket. "Well, do you want it then?" I shouted. "You might as well have it. It's not doing me any good."

"Put it away!" Freya hissed. She sounded angry, and it felt like I'd been slapped across the face.

"Why?" I asked.

"Because I could be one of them. Don't you understand? They want the Sikkilite, Sammel. They would kill you if they could."

"But they can't, can they? So, I've nothing to fear."

"I don't believe I'm having to explain this to you, Sammel. You're going to need to start thinking, and I mean really start thinking. No, they can't hurt you directly, but what they can do is much worse. They can make you think things, terrible things. And with those things they don't need to hurt you, because you'll start hurting yourself."

I didn't say anything for a moment. She was right. The demons affected the way I thought, and that was one of the most powerful things anyone could do. I remember hitting myself with the pebble on the beach. I put the Sikkilite back in my pocket.

"Are you there, Sammel?" Freya asked from the top bunk.

"I am."

"We're going to do this, okay? We're going to save me."

"There's only a couple of days left, and I don't know what I'm doing."

"You're doing just fine," Freya said. "Just fine."

The top bunk moved back up, and she was gone. Freya may not have been my girlfriend, but at that moment, lying alone in the cabin on the train, she was closest thing I had.

*

I didn't hear Bobby come in; the bed was soft and I was tired. All I know was that I could smell beer in the morning, even though he was no longer in the top bunk. I dressed in my new clothes and went along to the food car. Bobby was talking to a woman at one of the tables, so I grabbed some breakfast and ate alone.

The scenery had started to change now. It made me feel nostalgic. It made me feel old, too, but, unlike many people, I'd never had a problem with aging. The way I saw it, the only time you didn't get older was when you were dead.

I finished my breakfast and drank my tea. There was a newspaper in a rack, so I took it and skimmed through the headlines, which amounted to nothing much of anything. I looked at the number puzzles, but knew it was pointless, so turned my attention to the crossword. It killed some time. I'd expected Bobby to come over at some point, but he didn't appear.

*

If Freya hadn't been my girlfriend, then what had I been doing for the past two years? I tried to remember waking up in the mornings and seeing Freya asleep beside me, but, of course, I couldn't. She had never been there.

Yet, there were fragranced soaps, deodorants, female perfumes in the bathroom cabinet. Had I bought those? Had I been living some weird fantasy? What was wrong with me? And, more importantly, why wasn't I still thinking like that? What had changed which had allowed me to see some of my strangeness?

When I next looked out of the train window, Livia's mother was at the edge of a forest, watching me come back. I got my phone, and took a picture. When I looked at the image, the shape could have been a woman, but, then, it could have been anything.

The automated announcement system told us it was thirty minutes until we arrived at the destination. I stood and returned to our cabin, where Bobby was already packing things up.

"How ya feeling?" he asked.

"Strange."

"Me too."

I thought about showing him the photo I'd taken of Livia's mother, but didn't. This wasn't his problem.

"Who was the woman you were talking to?" I asked.

"No idea. We both just needed to do something."

We were silent then until the train pulled in at the station. We filed out and stood on the platform as it pulled away.

It was raining. Bobby tilted his face upwards and smiled.

"Feels good," he said. "How far to the house?"

"A few miles. I thought we might walk."

"You're the boss," Bobby said. "I go where you go."

"Are you sure you want to help me? You don't have to..."

"Shut the fuck up, and let's start walking."

*

There were taxis at the taxi rank, and for a moment I thought about changing my mind and getting one. Obviously, it'd be quicker, but at that moment I wasn't looking for speed. I wanted to relax, to find some sort of calmness before I reached my great aunt's house.

The rain didn't look like it was going to stop. Bobby was enjoying it; myself, less so. The scenery we passed was plain and nondescript. Drab houses lined the road with small box-shaped cars parked in their driveways. There were people around, though mostly they were on the other side of the road, heading in the opposite direction, towards the station. The clock on my phone told me it was eight thirty-four AM.

We stopped at a small convenience store, where we bought chocolate and drinks. The train food had been nice, but it hadn't been what we were used to. We sat on a wet bench outside the store and ate.

"How old are you?" Bobby asked me.

I shrugged. "Twenty-something."

"You don't know?"

"No."

"I saw that woman," he said. "The one you took a photograph of, out the window of the train."

"You saw her? Why didn't you say before?"

"Waiting to see if you wanted to. Guess you didn't."

"The photo didn't come out well. It could have been anything."

"Well, don't look up, but she's back."

"Where?"

"Through the gap in the houses over there. Looks like a park or something."

I took a second, then raised my head. Bobby was right. She was there, watching the two of us.

"What do you want to do?" he asked.

"Don't know. You got any ideas?"

"Any person who keeps showing up like this, must have something to say. I think we should go and talk to her."

I nodded. It made as much sense as everything else.

"But not yet," Bobby added. "I've not finished my chocolate yet."

*

The park grass was wet, and it didn't take long before my shoes were soaked through. The space was large, and partly filled with a playground for young children, and the obligatory skate ramps for the older ones. It could have been anywhere, in any city or town or village, in almost any country. The feeling of being lost, of being useless, returned.

Livia's mother didn't move. I had expected her to leave when we started towards her, but she remained solid and steadfast. She held up a hand to stop us, but Bobby kept walking.

"Hello," he said. "I'm Bobby. We've not had the pleasure."

Livia's mother didn't look at him.

"I appreciate you not wanting to talk to me," he continued. "But you don't have a choice, or haven't you realised that yet?"

Bobby stopped three yards in front of her.

"You've changed, Sammel," she said.

I wanted to reply, but Bobby gave me a look, which said he was handling this.

"What do you want?" he said. "It's got to be something, 'cause you're stalking us."

"Do you know what he did to me, the last time we met?"

Bobby shrugged. "Does it matter?"

"He smashed me into little pieces with a tennis racquet. That's not right, is it? That's hardly the actions of a normal person."

"I think we can both agree Sammel is not a normal person," Bobby said, with no hint of nastiness. "So, he tried to get rid of you. I'd have done the same thing. Tell me what you want?"

"I need you to find someone."

Bobby shook his head. "We've got more than enough tasks on our list, already."

"I'll make it worth your while."

"How?"

"Let me talk to Sammel."

"No. You talk to me. How can you help us?"

"I can help you find Freya. I know where she is."

"Why should we trust you?"

Livia's mother looked at Bobby for a long minute. Then her arm moved, and she threw something at the pair of us. Bobby bent and picked it up. It was a silk scarf. He turned and held it out in front of him so I could see it.

"This familiar to you?" he asked.

I nodded. "It's hers. Freya's. I can't say I remember seeing it before, but it's hers."

"Very well." He turned back to Livia's mother. "Okay, we'll help. Who is it you want us to find?"

"My daughter," Livia's mother said. "I need you to find Livia."

*

I stepped forward and put my hand on Bobby's arm. He took a step back.

"What happened to her?" I asked.

"Oh, so nice of you to join us, Sammel. She left school and disappeared. Went out one day and never came back."

I waited for something more, but she went quiet. She could have been making it up, throwing us off the scent, but I didn't know why she would bother.

"Last I remember," I said. "You were the expert on people who'd disappeared."

Anger flashed across her eyes.

"Do you think I haven't been looking for her all this time? She has gone, Sammel Ahlberg, and I think you might be able to get her back. You might be able to communicate with her, where I failed."

"Perhaps she's dead?"

"Aren't we all, in the end? Will you help?"

"Tell me how you know where Freya is?"

"I found her in my travels. That's all. Nothing clever about it."

"This makes no fucking sense," Bobby said, exasperated. "Why the fuck would we be successful where you weren't? We're not demons. We have no special powers."

"Sammel does. He has one very special power. He can travel to Songström at will. He can go there and find Livia."

"Songström isn't real," I told her.

"It's as real as the ground you're standing on, Sammel. Whatever else might be happening inside your mind, Songström is real."

I waited for a moment, thinking over Livia's mother's words.

"Okay," I told her. "I can go to Songström. But I have to travel to my great-aunt's first."

"Time is no obstacle for me," she said, with a flick of her hand.

I watched as she turned and retreated into the trees, her white gown growing indistinct behind the lattice of the woodland branches.

"Well, this gets easier by the fucking minute," Bobby said, sarcastically.

I smiled. "Doesn't it?"

*

By the time we arrived at great-aunt's house, we were both wet through.

"I'm going to wait out here," Bobby said. "Family stuff doesn't concern me."

I frowned at him, but let it go. He was right, this was my business.

I opened the gate to the house and went in. The pathway was narrow and overgrown, and at various places along its edge the concrete had begun to crumble away. The hedges lining the small front garden had grown tall and straggly, and the net curtains, which I always remember as shockingly white, were now a dull yellow.

It didn't look like anyone had lived there in a while.

*

I knocked lightly on the door and waited. A minute passed, so I knocked again. Still nothing. I cupped my hands above my eyes and peered through the window. All I could see through the gloom were the outlines of indistinguishable pieces of furniture.

I moved back off the front step, and looked at the upstairs windows; the curtains were all closed. I glanced to my right, where the path led off around the side of the house and on towards the back garden. I knew the way. I checked back to see if Bobby was all right, but the hedge blocked my view.

Alone, I made my way along the path beside the house, to the rotten gate, which stood between me and the back garden. Carefully, I placed my shoulder against it, pushed, and heard the bolt fall away on the other side.

*

Where once the back garden had been laid to lawn, now all that could be seen were tall grasses and rampant weeds.

In front of me, looming out of the greenery was a small brick shed. Seeing it again made me smile. It used to house the lawnmower, an old, lumbering petrol-powered thing, which I would beg my great-aunt to let me use.

She had refused my initial requests, citing my lack of experience. Then, after she had hurt her leg in a fall, she had to let me do it. I remembered her sitting out on the small concrete path that ran along the back of the house, watching me go up and down, a broad smile on my face. She wouldn't say anything. I'd carry on until it ran out of petrol, then refill it, and start all over again.

When her leg became too much to cope with, one of her friends had come to stay, and there hadn't really been room for me anymore.

*

I pulled on the door of the brick shed and it opened. There, in-between the grime and the cobwebs, sat the lawnmower.

It looked at me. 'Where've you been?'

"Away," I replied, and it understood. Everyone must go.

"Fill me up one more time," it asked, and I saw the can of petrol nearby.

*

When I'd finished, I said goodbye and pushed my way through to where I knew the back door was. It was wooden and just as rotten as the gate had been. I'd been ready to force it open, but noticed it was already unlocked, so simply twisted the handle, and wiggled it until there was a big enough gap for me to fit through. The smell from inside was awful.

I found my torch and switched it on.

The internal fixtures of the kitchen were exactly how I remembered them, apart from the addition of two rats; one on the table and one in the corner by the sideboard.

I gave the rodents a wide berth, and inspected the worktop, which was littered with rat faeces. Next to it, the sink was stacked high with unwashed and mouldy plates, and next to that, a larder. There was no point looking in there. Nothing good would come of that.

I walked into the stubby hallway, where the wallpaper, rotten and dark was peeling away from the black walls underneath. A table still stood against the wall to the right, a mirror over the top of it.

"I don't want to be here," I said, quietly.

*

The front room door had come away from its topmost hinge. Beyond it, everything was decaying. Furniture sagged, the carpet was threadbare, and the ceiling bowed at one side.

The house was derelict. Not just derelict. Dangerous. It was stupid to have come here. I should have guessed she wouldn't be here. Who would...

There was a noise on the floor above me. A cough, perhaps. I walked to the bottom of the stairs, and looked up.

"Great-aunt?" I called.

A recognisable cough, this time. She was trying to clear her throat.

"Sammel?" came a weak voice.

"Yes, it's Sammel."

A pause. "Why are you here?"

"I've come back, great-aunt. I want to ask you some questions."

"You shouldn't be here."

"I need to know about my father."

"I owe you nothing, Sammel Ahlberg. Get out."

I felt a wave of anger pass through me. What was the matter with her? I just had one question to ask.

I put my foot on the bottom step, and began to climb.

"Go away!" she shouted. "Go away!"

"Where is my father?"

"In the ground. In the ground, and safe from you!"

I was halfway up the stairs already, my hand gripping the bannister tightly.

"Why do you say that?"

A laugh then, her laugh. "Huh, no one else could see it, Sammel. But I saw it. I saw the sort of person you were!"

I was almost at the top now.

"Where is he, great-aunt? Where's my father?"

"I'm not going to tell you. He didn't want me to tell you."

I was outside her bedroom door.

"Where is he?" I growled.

No answer. Then, from somewhere, a 'wumph!' I knew that sound. A fire igniting. I smelt the petrol, then, a strong smell wafting up from downstairs.

I twisted the door handle, it was locked. I drew my leg back and kicked hard against the plyboard. The door shot inwards, and I saw my great-aunt for the first time in years.

*

She'd asked me to leave. I suppose that was the truth of it. I'd outstayed my welcome, outstayed it by a long way.

She'd always blamed me for the fall, but it hadn't been my fault, not directly. She'd tripped on the same stairs I'd just walked up. I hadn't even been in the house, but it hadn't stopped her blaming me.

The day I'd left, there'd been a knock on the front door. People rarely visited. She'd had friends, but they'd come around less and less since I'd been living there.

I hadn't answered the door. They weren't my friends. Then I'd heard the key in the lock, and the front door had opened.

I'd gone to the top of the stairs.

"Who is it?" I'd said.

I could see their shape, large and broad, filling the hallway. Great-aunt appeared from her room.

"It's time to go," she'd said. "I've packed your bags."

I'd thought about fighting, about resisting, but I wouldn't win. I'd looked at her, and then at the bag which was sat in the hallway downstairs, and I'd nodded.

"Goodbye," I said.

She didn't reply. I remembered her standing there, defiant, at the last.

*

Now, she stood again, in the centre of the room. She appeared just as I remembered her. Only, this wasn't her room any more. This was Songström, and she stood in the lounge of the middle house.

"Why are you here? Why are you in Songström?"

"I owe you no explanation, Sammel. I owe you nothing."

There was a banging on the front door.

"Sammel?" Bobby shouted. "Get the fuck out, it's on fire!"

"Tell me about my father," I pleaded. "I have to know."

"Enough to die for it?" she asked. "Would you die to know?"

"Yes, yes I would."

"Give me the Sikkilite," she said. "And I'll tell you."

I took it out of my pocket and stepped into her room.

"Here it is," I said, holding it out in front of me.

The sight of it must've been too much. Great-aunt launched herself at it. I grabbed her arm and threw her out of the room, onto the landing. A dark shadow appeared over the house, swooping low.

I stepped out of Songström, and I closed the door. Great-aunt lay sprawled by the top of the stairs.

"Why did you do that? Why did you take me out of Songström?"

"Tell me about my father and I'll send you back there."

"You bastard, Sammel Ahlberg."

"Tell me!"

She cowered, and I felt slightly guilty.

"He's alive, all right. He didn't die. He just didn't come back. Was worried the illness would return if he saw you again."

My father was still alive? I should have been angry. I should have been hurt.

"Perhaps he was right," I said. There was a silence then, just for a moment.

"Send me back," Great-aunt said.

"Where is he now?"

"The illness returned a year ago, and so did he. He tried to find you. He wanted to see you before he went. Too late, though. Too late."

"He's dead?"

Bobby's shouts drifted up from below. "The fucking house is burning down, Sammel! Get out!"

"No. He's in the hospice. There's not much time. A couple of days, maybe."

I stepped over her and started down the stairs. "Thank you,"

"Send me back to Songström! You said you would."

The smoke was thick in the hallway. I opened the front door, and the two rats from the kitchen ran out through my legs.

I turned back and saw her trying to crawl down the stairs. "You'll be there, soon enough," I said. "I promise."

*

Bobby was on the path outside. "Get the fuck out of there!" he shouted, above the sound of the flames. "For fuck's sake, Sammel!"

I stepped over the threshold, closing the door behind me.

"Thank you," I told him.

"Do I have to save your backside every time?"

I shrugged. "There isn't anyone else."

"We need to get the fuck out of here, before the police arrive. No way we can explain this!"

Quietly, we left via a side street, that would keep us hidden from prying eyes, and from there, made our way into the centre of town, such as it was. I looked back once, but all I could see was the smoke.

"Do you think she'll be all right?" I asked Bobby.

"The dead person?"

"Yes."

"I guess you've done her a favour."

*

We found a café and sat at a table for two. I ordered a latte, but Bobby said he didn't want anything. The waitress smiled, and walked off behind the counter.

"So, can you do it then?"

"Do what?"

"Go to this Songström place at will."

"Up till now, it's tended to find me," I said. "But I might be able to."

Bobby looked at me, expectantly. I knew why; I just didn't want to ask.

"Well, come on," he said. "We're going to have to try at some point."

"After the coffee," I said. "Coffee comes first."

The interior of the café was modern, with mirrors of different shapes and sizes hung around the walls. I didn't much like looking in mirrors. The face that looked back never felt like my own.

I watched the waitress make my drink in the well-practised manner of someone who's been doing their job too long. She looked over once and smiled, and I immediately dropped my gaze.

"That's not how you communicate with the fairer sex," Bobby said, under his breath.

I ignored him. We couldn't all be Bobby, yet I did my best to smile at her when she brought the coffee over.

"Thank you," I croaked.

"Would you like anything to eat, at all?" she asked, even though I'd said no the last time.

"Um..." I started. Bobby nudged my leg under the table. "Perhaps something warm. A toasted sandwich? Do you have one of those?"

She smiled, wider this time. "Yes, I'll make one for you."

"That's more like it," Bobby said, as she walked away.

"She probably just feels sorry for me."

"So what?" Bobby said. "It doesn't matter how you get talking."

"It does, if she thinks I'm a loser."

I sugared, stirred and sipped my coffee.

"So, are you mad at him?" Bobby said.

"My father? No. Not in the slightest."

"But he left you thinking he was dead."

"Yes, and for all intents and purposes, he was. He was living in another country, with another chance at life. Who am I to deny him the opportunity to take it?"

"I think I'd be more fucking upset than that."

"Well, I'm not."

"Thought what you're going to say to him?"

203

"Why should I? He might not want to see me."

"Well, if he doesn't, he's going to have me to deal with."

"Perhaps," I said. "Perhaps I won't let you come in."

"I need a beer," Bobby said. "Don't you?"

"No."

The café was empty, and I wondered where everyone else was. We'd been there fifteen minutes or so, and there hadn't been another customer.

"I need a piss," Bobby said, and stalked off in the direction the toilet sign indicated. The waitress lifted a handle and took out the toasted sandwich. She put it on a plate and walked over.

"Here you are," she said.

"Thank you. That's, er, that's what I ordered."

The waitress hovered by the table for a moment. I guessed it must be boring being here when it's empty.

"It's not very busy today." I said.

She looked out the front window. "I think the weather is putting them off."

"That's a shame."

She smiled.

"Do you mind if I sit down?"

"Not at all."

She sat in the chair Bobby had been using.

"Can't be much to do on days like this?"

"Not really," she said. "I write when there's nothing to do. I've got a pad of paper behind the counter, and if no one's in, or needs serving, I just get on with the story I'm writing."

"What story's that?" I asked.

"I don't like talking about it."

"That's okay. I understand," I told her. "I try and keep things I'm doing close to my chest. I'm always worried I might not finish them if I tell someone."

She sat up ever so slightly when I said that. Her mouth smiled even wider, and a little light seemed to appear behind her eyes. "That's exactly it," she said. "Oh, I'm glad someone else thinks the same. I was beginning to think I was a little weird."

"Weird is okay."

She nodded. "Good." She stuck out her hand. "I'm Sophia."

"Oh," I said. "I'm Sammel."

"All the esses," she said. I nodded, then after a moment realised what she'd meant.

"Yes, all the esses."

There was a pause then. There was always a pause. Usually, it would have happened a lot sooner than this.

"What are you doing here?" she asked.

"I'm visiting. I used to live here."

"Really? Whereabouts?"

I pointed in a general direction. "Over there somewhere."

She laughed. She thought I was being funny, where, in fact, I was just trying not to tell her I lived in the house that was currently burning to the ground with a demon inside it, who used to be my great-aunt. I was glad for the misdirection.

"Are you going back home today?"

"I'm not sure. I might be. I might not. Are there any nice places to stay?"

"There's an inn, The Blackbird, one road over. It generally has rooms available. And of course, a bar."

"Thank you. If my visit runs over, I'll check it out."

"Do. Well, I should let you to eat, Sammel. It was nice meeting you."

"And you," I replied.

Sophia stood and walked away, straightening her black dress.

The toasted sandwich was good, and didn't turn into fat white maggots. My phone buzzed in my pocket, and when I looked at it, I'd received a message from Bobby, reading, 'Slipped out whilst you were talking, you old devil. Will meet you in The Blackbird at eight PM."

That was good. I hadn't wanted to go to Songström, not before I'd spoken to Sophia, and definitely not after. Whenever I went there, things always got confusing, and I didn't want Sophia to be caught up in it.

The door opened behind me, and I thought perhaps Bobby had returned. I waited for the pat on the shoulder, perhaps the odd cussing as he approached. Instead someone sat on the table behind me, facing my back. It was a strange place to sit considering the emptiness of the place.

Sophia looked up from the counter. I could tell she'd been writing. She put her pen down, and stood. I started to panic. I didn't want her to serve them. Whoever it was, they didn't feel right. Sophia straightened her dress once more, and picked up her notepad. I stood, and walked towards her, smiling as we got closer.

"Is everything all right?" she asked.

I nodded. "Can I ask you a question? At the counter?"

She looked confused, and I didn't blame her. "At the counter?"

"Yes. I know it's weird, but it's like you not telling me your story. Do you see?"

"A little bit."

She turned and made her way back there. I followed, blocking out any images in the mirrors that were trying to catch the corner of my eye. When we reached the counter, she turned to face me, a lopsided grin on her face.

"What's the matter, Sammel?"

"The person who just walked in, can you describe them to me?"

"Really? That's what you wanted to ask me?"

"Please. It's important."

Sophia gasped. "Are you on the run? Is it the police?"

I shook my head. "It's not the police," I told her. "On the contrary. They're the bad guys."

"The bad guys," Sophia said. "Is this some sort of game?"

"Kind of."

"Well, in that case," she said. "It's a male, about your height. Short cropped hair. Jeans and a shirt."

"What about his face? What does it look like?"

Sophia looked, squinted, then shook her head, confused. "I can't tell," she said. "I don't understand, Sammel. Why can't I see what he looks like?"

"Does he have no face? Nothing inside his head at all?" Sophia concentrated her stare and then gasped. I grabbed her hand. "Look at me," I told her. "Look right at me."

She turned her head. "What's happening?"

"They can't hurt us. They're just here to scare us."

"Where's its face, Sammel? I feel sick."

"Don't worry about it. Don't think about it. Keep looking at me. Is there another way out of here?"

"Yes. There's a back door."

"I want you to take me there, now. Got it?"

"But I can't leave the café, I'd lose my job."

"I'll vouch for you. Please. We need to leave now."

She nodded. "Okay," she said. "Follow me."

Sophia took my hand and led me around the side of the counter. "Don't look in the mirrors," I told her. "Don't even glimpse."

She did as I said. We passed by the toilets, where Bobby had gone, and towards another door, marked with a 'Fire Exit' sign.

"It's through here," Sophia said. Her hands were shaking. My anger rose. Why did it try and destroy everything? Why did Songström not want me to have friends?

Sophia pushed the bar on the door, and it swung open, away from us. We stepped out into the middle of the three huts. I turned around, but before I'd had chance to react, the door had disappeared, and we were back in Songström proper.

*

"Stay still," I said to Sophia. "Don't panic."

"What the hell just happened? Why isn't it raining? Where the hell are we?"

"It's what they wanted us to do. They wanted us to run. We've been set up."

"Set up? How?"

"This place. It feeds off of fear and sadness. Don't go near the buildings."

I watched Sophia. She was bewildered, unable to process everything that had happened to her over the last few minutes.

"We could run," she whispered. "Through the gaps between the huts."

"And go where? There might places much worse than this beyond them."

Sophia rounded on me. She gripped my forearms. "Who are you, really?" she said, anger and fear mixed in her eyes.

"I'm Sammel Ahlberg," I told her. "I'm no one special."

"That's bullshit. I believe everything happens for a reason. You've been brought here for a reason. To do something. What is it, Sammel?"

"I don't know," I said. "I don't know why it wants me."

Sophia slapped me hard across the face. I stopped everything. Moving, talking, thinking. It hurt, but I immediately knew why she'd done it.

"I'm here because I thought I was looking for my girlfriend. But she isn't my girlfriend. I don't know who she is, but whoever she is, it has something to do with this place."

"That's better."

"And there's something else. I have a stone. She, Freya, called it Sikkilite, but I think it's just Onyx or something."

I took it out of my pocket, and opened my palm. Sophia peered at the black stone, keeping her distance.

"What's it supposed to do?" she asked.

"Freya told me it would keep her soul safe. But it was a lie, because she wasn't who she said she was."

It went dark for a moment, as if something was swooping down, blocking out the sun.

"We have to get out of here," I told Sophia.

"No."

"What? We have to get out."

"No," Sophia said. "If you keep running away you'll never be free of it. We have to stand our ground."

I looked into the sky but couldn't see the blackness.

"I don't know what'll happen."

"That doesn't mean you shouldn't find out."

The blackness swooped once more, lower this time.

"Do you see it? The dark?"

"I see it. But I see you, too."

We stood, facing each other. I'd never been so frightened. This was not a place to be lost in. We wouldn't be found again, I was sure of it.

There was another voice. "Get out!" A woman's voice.

"Freya?" I called.

"Get out!"

"Great-aunt?"

"Get out!"

"Mother?"

And then she appeared in front of me. Not as I remembered her, because I didn't remember her. Since the day she'd died, my mother had been little more than a feeling. A safe feeling.

"Sammel," she said.

"I see them, mother. I see the demons, too."

"I know. They used you to give them more power. It's not your fault. I was weak through alcohol, and it cost me everything. You're stronger than I was. You can fight them. You can't defeat Songström, this place is here whether you exist or not, but you can stop them coming after you. Do you have the Sikkilite?"

"I do." I felt stupid then. This was the one thing that almost belonged here. If anything was to have any power, any usefulness in this domain, it'd be the Sikkilite.

I took it from my pocket.

"Do you remember whose it was?"

I looked at her. Something cracked, inside my head, and a shaft of light, yellowed with time, crept through the gap.

That time. That time when I heard the scream and I ran to help Livia. But I wasn't helping Livia, I was helping my mother. Livia was the one who had the fork in her hand. My mother trying to hold her off.

And there, strapped around her throat with the leather bootlace, was the Sikkilite.

"It was yours," I said. "You had it around your throat."

"I showed your father. I asked him to come and save me, and when I stopped talking, I saw you standing in the bedroom doorway, looking in."

"Why didn't he save you?"

"He tried. And the trying made him sick, Sammel. Your father tried, and almost lost his life."

"Is it too late for you to use it?" I asked.

"It's never too late," she said. "The sun never sets here, it's a single day, forever. But I don't need saving, Sammel. Not anymore."

"Then what should I do with it?"

"Take it to your father. He's the one who needs it now."

The darkness swooped down again, and everything was black, and when it was light again, we were in the café, and I was sitting at the table. Sophia sat on the stool by the counter, pen in hand looking at her notebook.

*

For a moment, I thought it'd never happened. I thought my mind had created everything, and I was just living a lie that never ended. Then I saw Sophia's face change to confusion. She put the pen down slowly, and looked up at me. There was terror in her eyes. I recognised that terror. I had been a young boy when I'd first experienced it.

"Sammel," she half-whispered. She looked unsteady, as if she might topple off the stool.

I stood and walked towards her. "It was real, Sophia."

Before I reached her, the door opened behind me. I tensed, was about to turn, and fight.

"We're closed," said Sophia, calmly and steadily. The door opened and closed again.

"I'm sorry," I said to Sophia.

"No, I'm sorry," she said. She stood, raised her arms and hugged me.

I held her. I couldn't remember the last time I'd held anybody. She stepped back and looked at me.

"Do you have that Sikkilite thing?" I opened my hands. I was still holding it. "Amazing," she said.

"Am I mad?" I said to Sophia.

"I don't think so," she replied. "I might be. You could be just a figment of my imagination. How do you feel about that?"

"Fine, but perhaps you could think some nice things for me, now?"

Sophia smiled. "I'll try. That lady mentioned your father. Where is he?"

"In a hospice, near here."

Sophia's body language changed. She had a purpose. "Come on, then. We need to go and see him."

"What about the café."

"Sod the café," she said. "Sod all of this."

I laughed. Looked at her and laughed. "Thank you," I told her.

"Don't thank me, yet."

*

Sophia closed the café. "I hate this place," she said as she turned the key. "When the hell did my dreams become regular lattes and pain-au-chocolates?"

We walked quickly. I looked around for Bobby, but he wasn't anywhere to be found.

The streets began to thin, and the houses began to grow. It was close to lunchtime.

I knew about the hospice, but could never remember visiting. It was purpose-built, a place for people to be cared for when care was all they needed. The doors swished open as we approached; swished closed behind us. The reception desk was only a few paces away.

Sophia slowed down. "Go on," she said.

"Aren't you coming in?"

"You hardly know me."

"I don't want to lose sight of you. I know it sounds stupid. But when I lose sight of people, sometimes they don't come back."

"Okay," she said. "If you're sure."

"Please."

We approached the reception desk together. The receptionist smiled.

"Hello," she said.

"Hi. I'm here to see my father."

"What's the name?"

"Mats. Mats Ahlberg."

She frowned slightly. "I don't remember seeing that name," she said, not unkindly. "Is he new?"

I shrugged. "I don't know. I only just found out he was here."

She looked at the computer screen beside her. Typed the name 'Ahlberg' and hit a button labelled 'Search'. The resulting screen read 'No Results Found'.

"Right. Do you think he might be under a different name?"

"I guess. He moved away when I was young. He might have changed it."

Sophia leant in a little closer. "Do you have anyone with the first name of Sammel?"

She turned back to the screen, and typed in 'Sammel'. She hit 'Search'. The screen read '2 Results Found'. She clicked on the first one. A man's face appeared. She turned the screen towards us slightly.

"Could this be him?"

I remembered back to Moby. I could remember the demon better than I could remember my father. I pictured the tennis racquet in his mouth, me taking it back to the house, and my father's face lighting up.

"Yes," I said. "Yes, I think that's him."

"He looks like you," Sophia said.

"He said he was expecting someone," the receptionist replied. "Well, normally we don't allow visitors in at lunchtime, but I think today we can bend the rules a little."

She called a man in uniform over, and he showed us the way to a day room, which was empty apart from some chairs, a low table, and some pictures of the sea on the wall.

"Wait here," he said, and left.

Sounds of lunchtime could be heard beyond the room. Clinking of plates, movement of people as they were taken to the dining area, and the hubbub of chatter.

I was nervous, my leg involuntarily bobbing up and down.

"It'll be all right," Sophia said.

The door opened and a man was wheeled into the room, a drip attached to his arm. He was thin, and weak, but he looked at me and smiled.

"Sammel," he said. "I wondered if I'd get to see you."

"I didn't know you were still alive."

It was hard to embrace a man with a drip in his arm. I leant in, awkwardly, and he did the same. We met somewhere in the middle.

"I had no choice. I couldn't let you know. If you'd known, then they'd have come after you."

"Who?"

"The demons."

"They found me, anyway."

There was the briefest of silences.

"Who's this?" he asked.

"This is my friend, Sophia."

"Pleased to meet you."

"Likewise," she said. "Sammel has something for you."

My father turned his head back towards me. "Oh, yes?"

I produced the Sikkilite, and his eyes widened.

"Where did you get that?"

"I've always had it, I think. Looked after it. I'm supposed to give it to you."

"Yes," he agreed, reaching up a shaking arm and taking it from me.

"What does it do?" I asked. "I mean, what does it really do?"

"I think it's a marker, Sammel. I think it allows us to travel somewhere whole, and not be broken up by the ghosts. Have you met ghosts?"

I nodded. "Yes," I told him. "One of them helped me."

"They aren't to be trusted," he mumbled. He looked sad, suddenly. "I thought I could trust them..."

"I saw mother," I said, and that brought his gaze back to me.

"That's good."

"She was in Songström."

His face darkened.

"Songström needs to be destroyed, Sammel."

"Destroyed? But... mother said it would always be there."

"What it represents will always be there, but Songström is yours. It's personal. You went there once, didn't you? Walked there when you were younger, went into the huts?"

"Yes, but I never told you."

"I wanted to shelter you from it, Sammel. I didn't want you going back. I wanted you to think it was all in your head. But it was a mistake. It needs to be burnt to the ground."

"But mother's there."

"No. She isn't. It's just a place through which she can talk to you. It needs to go, Sammel. Songström will destroy you, don't think it won't. Don't think it's not trying to find a way to get at you right now, to make you give in, and give up. Songström won't ever leave you alone. It took your mother, and in my grief, it took me. You must be stronger, even if being stronger means letting go of all of this."

He turned to Sophia. "You will help him?"

"Of course," she said.

"The struggle is to the death, Sammel, as all of life is. Songström may not be the war, but it's a battle. And an important one."

"We will destroy it, if that is what has to be done," I said to my father.

"Good. I have faith you will."

My father looked tired. He twisted the Sikkilite cord in his hands.

"Father?"

"Yes?"

"Who's Freya?"

"Freya?" His brow furrowed as he thought about the name. "I don't know. I've not heard you mention the name before. Is she important?"

"I think so. I think she's part of Songström, somehow. I just don't know what part."

"We're all a part of Songström," he said. "It's just that most of us don't know it." He put the Sikkilite in his lap, and put up his arms. "Farewell son," he said. "I'm sorry we didn't spend more time together."

I bent and held him. "Don't be sorry. You gave me everything you could. I'm proud of you."

"And I of you. Be on the lookout for your old dad, eh?" I thought he was going to let me go, but instead he moved his mouth closer to my ear. "There's someone waiting for you outside," he whispered. I pulled back and frowned. "You'll see." He reached his thin arm behind him and knocked on the door. It opened, and the man who showed us into the room came in and wheeled him out. I walked at the same pace, watching as he was taken down the hall.

Just before he went into the lunchroom, he touched the sleeve of the man pushing him, who stopped the wheelchair. My father turned and looked at me.

"You don't remember the phone call, do you, Sammel?"

I thought for a moment, then shook my head. "What phone call?"

He smiled. "Never mind," he said, and motioned for the man to continue.

Sophia stood beside me.

"You don't have to help," I said to her.

"I know. But I want to. Sometimes you've got to grab the chances when you can."

I looked at her and smiled. "Then, we should go."

*

I went back through reception, and through the swishing doors. Sitting at the entrance to the car park, where my father said someone would be waiting, was Moby, tail wagging and tennis racquet in his mouth. Sophia couldn't see him, but she was willing to accept he was there. I described him to her, and she said hello, which only made the demon wag his tail more.

"He likes you," I told her.

"I never doubted it," she replied. I looked at Sophia for a moment.

"Do I know you?" I asked her. "I mean, have we met before this?"

"Well, if you grew up here, then there's always a chance."

"Yes, I suppose there is."

She smiled. "What happens next?"

I looked at Moby. The racquet had gone and he was lying on the ground.

"Well, we still have to find Livia, and since we have Moby, perhaps he could sniff her out?"

"Yes, that actually makes sense in a weird way," she said. "We'll probably need something of hers so he can get the scent."

I nodded.

"We should go to where they lived. It was a few doors down from our old house."

"Well, I have a car. If you like, I could drive?"

"It'd be really out of your way."

"I know."

*

The rain was beginning to ease, and there were even a couple of clear patches in the sky. We walked back towards the café, and Sophia retrieved her car. Moby walked a few paces behind us, looking left and right, watching, protecting.

It was good to have him back, and I wished Sophia could see him. After her brush with Songström, I'd hoped she might be able to.

She drew the car up next to us. It was blue. I let Moby in the back, then opened the passenger's door and got in.

"Lead on," she said, and put the car into gear.

*

The place where I grew up was a twelve-hour drive away. I suggested to Sophia that we stopped halfway, and I could pay for a room for the night, and she agreed.

Sophia liked to drive with the car radio on, and as we travelled through the countryside, we listened to a variety of music. It was nice. I rarely listened to music.

The DJs were good company, too. They'd change, as we'd move out of the reach of one station and into the realms of another. Each had their own style, with some being loud and brash, and others quiet and intimate. It was interesting. Soothing.

Sophia's car became a place of safety. She asked me what town she should head towards and I told her, then she suggested I should get some rest. I moved the car seat back, reclined it, and was asleep within a couple of minutes, helped by the rocking of the car.

*

I dreamed a different dream. The movement of the car became the lull of the ocean, and I was lying on my back, floating on the top of the water. There were stars in the sky, and the moon was a crescent.

I looked around. To the left was the pier, to the right, nothing but coastline and waves.

I could hear the music from the car radio seeping through, and the sounds of the presenter mumbling low, as if they were beneath the water.

I spread my arms out to my sides as far as they would go. The water was warm. Everything felt good.

Then, my right hand brushed against something cold, and I started.

I woke, still feeling the coldness. I looked down and realised my hand was resting on the handbrake. That was all it'd been. I looked at Sophia, and she had a frown on her face.

"Everything all right?" she asked.

"Yes, just a dream."

We arrived at the halfway point around seven in the evening. There was a nondescript hotel which charged too much for the quality of the rooms, so we ventured a little further into town, and found a small, family-run alternative we were both happy with. We put everything we'd brought with us into the room, then went out in search of somewhere to eat.

We found an Italian restaurant that was open, and were shown to a table near the window. Sophia went off to the bathroom, so I dug my phone out of my bag and replied to Bobby's message, saying I couldn't get to the pub and telling him where we were. His reply consisted of a 'thumbs up' picture and a winking face. He didn't seem to mind.

I ordered pizza and Sophia ordered spaghetti, which smelt nice when it arrived.

"I like it here," she said. "There's something quaint about everything."

The waiter appeared with a bottle of wine.

"We didn't order wine," I told him.

Sophia put her hand on my arm. "My treat," she said. "I ordered it at the bar a moment ago. I hope that was all right."

I smiled. "It's fine," I said. "I just don't usually drink alcohol."

The waiter poured and we drank. It was good. I finished the first glass before I realised it.

"Sorry," I told Sophia, who simply smiled, and poured me another.

"Why are you being so nice to me?" I asked her. "No one's ever nice to me."

"Why shouldn't I be nice to you? I saw Songström," she replied. "And it's scary. You need all the help you can get."

"It's hard being me," I told her, sipping from the glass. "To be in my head. Seeing what I see and hearing what I hear. I've been alone for a long time."

"We all have worlds inside our heads," Sophia said. "Some are more filled-out than others, but it doesn't mean you have to be alone with them. Speaking about them will help."

*

I slept on the left bed and Sophia slept on the right. At one point during the night, I woke to see a shadow of a woman sitting near the window, wisps of smoke around her head, but I didn't do anything, because I didn't believe it was real. I rolled onto my side and I looked at Sophia sleeping quietly, and I felt calmed.

*

In the morning, we went for breakfast. I was hungry, and slightly hungover. It felt good. It felt like I might have lived a day at last.

We were in the car by ten AM, and crossed the border around midday. Everything felt different. I was getting closer to the place where Songström existed in the real world.

Sophia remained quiet. She was happy to let me think, every now and again breaking into song if the radio played one of her favourites. It was nice to listen to. She had a pretty voice that reminded me of something I couldn't quite remember.

We ate lunch at two PM in the car.

"Is Moby okay?" she asked. I looked in the back.

"It seems fine," I said. The dog was lying in the footwell. It wasn't asleep. I'd never seen Moby asleep. I'd never seen any demon sleep.

*

At three-fifteen PM, we stopped at the end of the road where I used to live.

"What happened here?" Sophia asked. I got out of the car and looked.

"I don't know."

There were big concrete blocks across the road, and beyond, houses smothered by gardens left alone to grow out of control.

I opened the car's back door, and Moby got out. Sophia got out, too, and locked the vehicle.

"It's like the world ended, here," she said. "It makes me feel sad."

I nodded, and, together, we climbed over the concrete barriers and walked in.

*

"It looks like subsidence, but on a massive scale," Sophia said, as we stood at the edge of one of the many large holes that littered the road, gardens, and houses of the street. "Why didn't they just tear the whole place down? Or repair it?"

"I don't know."

Moby put his head down and sniffed at the fissure to the left of us.

"It's interested in this one," I said, and walked across. We gathered around its edge and stared down. It was deep, disappearing down into blackness.

"Shouldn't the fences be higher?" Sophia asked, looking back at the concrete blocks.

"They don't need to be. I don't expect anyone wants to come here."

"Look," she said, pointing in the direction of the houses. There was a light on in an upstairs window of a house I recognised. The house had a hole in its roof. "Is that Livia's house?"

"No," I replied. "Not Livia's. That's my old house. And that's my mother's room."

*

I skirted the hole and walked up the path to my old front door. The house wasn't burnt; whenever these craters had appeared, it was after it had been rebuilt. The door was open, the lock jimmied

227

off. I supposed all the houses had been looted in this way, including Livia's. My heart sank a little when I realised we'd be lucky to find anything of hers that might help Moby find her.

I pushed at my old front door, and listened to the creak as it swung back on its hinges. Sophia had stopped at the gate behind me, and I turned to look at her.

"Do you want me to wait here?" she asked.

"Yes. If that's okay? I'm not sure what I'm going to find."

"Of course. Just shout if you need me. And... good luck."

I nodded and turned away from Sophia. The inside of the house was lit with what little afternoon sun was permeating the clouds. It was better than no sun at all, I supposed, but it did little to dent my fear of facing whatever might be waiting for me upstairs. I took a deep breath, clenched my fists, and walked to the bottom of the staircase.

I remembered the day I'd had to run up it, and had thought I was helping Livia by hitting my mother with the lamp. I'd thought I'd escaped this place forever. In truth, I wanted to leave; to run. I wanted to return to the supermarket, and to the café. I wanted to be Sammel Ahlberg, who bought his monthly magazine and bothered no one.

"Mother?" I called.

"I'm here, Sammel. Come on up when you're ready."

I climbed the stairs, holding onto the slippery bannister, testing each step as I went, making sure they could take my weight. At the top, I turned and walked to the second door on the left; her bedroom door. I could see the light coming from under it. It'd been so long since I'd been here. How many years, I wondered. How old had I been? How old was I now? I put out my hand and knocked gently, twice, like it was the beginning of an old joke.

"Come in, Sammel," she said.

I put my palm on the handle, and was surprised by its coldness. I had an instant flashback to the dream in the car. I twisted the handle and pushed open the door.

*

My mother was lying in her bed, the sheets pulled up to her chin. "Hello, Sammel," she said. "It's good to see you. I've been waiting for you."

I looked around the room. It was undamaged, identical to all those times I had sneaked a peek at it when I'd been young.

"I never thought I'd be back here," I told her.

"Of course not," she said.

"What happened outside? All the holes?"

"Songström got too powerful here. The grief turned inwards, collapsed the world a little. People died, Sammel. People died when the holes appeared. And do you know what that meant?"

"No," I told her.

"It meant the holes just got bigger. In the end, there was no one left, and no one came back. They might not have known why they never returned, but it didn't matter. It worked, and Songström was powerless to do more damage."

"I'm looking for Livia," I said. "Or something that will lead me to her. Her mother's trying to find her."

"Pah, you can't trust any of them, you know that?"

"I do, but I'm looking for someone myself, and they said they could help."

"Who are you looking for?"

"A woman by the name of Freya. Have you heard that name?"

She thought, then shook her head. "No."

"Livia's mother says she can help me find her, but only if I help her find Livia."

"I can tell you where Livia is," my mother said. "But first, perhaps you can tell me something."

"If I can."

"How is your father? I miss him so much."

"Not well. He's close to the end."

"Does he have the Sikkilite?"

"He does."

She closed her eyes when I said this, and I thought I could make out a smile.

"Then I will be able to find him. I'm so looking forward to seeing him again."

"Can you tell me where Livia is?" I asked.

"She's down the hole in the road outside. The big one. One second she was there, the next she had gone. Good riddance to the demon, that's what I say. Good riddance to her."

I almost laughed. Of course, Livia was down the hole. Moby had already known it.

"I have to go and find her," I said. "I think things are coming to an end."

"Then be careful. I don't know where the hole goes, but it's not going to be anywhere nice."

"I'll be careful."

I looked at my mother, and she smiled at me. "Can you do one last thing for me, Sammel?"

"What's that?"

"When you leave, can you turn out the light?"

I looked around the room, but couldn't see where the light was coming from.

"I'm not sure how," I said.

"Look inside yourself. Deep inside. That's where it's coming from. Always was."

I nodded. "Of course," I said. I walked over and took my mother's hand. "I love you," I told her. "And I miss you very much."

"And I miss you. Sorry I wasn't much of a parent."

"We are always more than we think we are. And you more than most."

I bent and kissed her on the forehead.

"See you soon," I told her. She squeezed my hand. I turned and when I was at the door, the light went out.

*

I walked down the stairs, along the hallway and out to where Sophia and Moby were waiting.

"Everything okay?" she asked.

"Getting there," I said. "I think, at last, I'm getting there."

*

We stood at the edge of the large hole.

"It'd be madness to go down," Sophia said, and she had a point.

"It's where Livia is."

Moby barked. It'd been looking at me ever since I'd come out of the house. I knew why.

"Moby wants to go down," I told her. "I'm not sure if it should."

"Well, he's probably the best equipped of all of us," Sophia said. "We could give him an hour, and then go down after it?"

"All right," I agreed. I looked at Moby. "Go on, then."

The dog stepped onto the slope and slid. Sophia laughed and pointed to the pieces of gravel and earth that were toppling as Moby made its way down.

"It feels like everything I ever thought doesn't matter anymore," she said. "Like discovering today is the first day you're truly alive."

I laughed, Moby barked.

At the bottom of the slope, before it fell away completely, Moby dug in and looked around.

"Change," I shouted at it. He barked again, and then slowly the bark became a scream, and the dog became the demon, and then was gone.

Sophia took my hand and we sat with our backs against my old front garden wall, waiting.

*

Two hours had passed by the time I heard the scream start to return. Sophia was asleep, head resting on my shoulder. I tapped her gently on the leg, and she blinked herself awake.

"Moby's coming back."

We pushed ourselves up and waited near the hole. Underneath the screaming, I could hear another noise. Muffled at first, but then gradually changing into a girl's unhappy shouts.

"Get off me, mutt!" she yelled.

"There," Sophia said, and pointed to the right of centre. I looked and saw Moby pulling at a girl's arm. The girl was wearing dark clothing,

"I can see them," Sophia said.

"It must be Songström. As it gets stronger, it becomes more real."

233

The girl, Livia, looked up at us.

"Oh, the boy from three doors down," she said, her voice heavy with sarcasm. "I thought I'd seen the last of you. And who's this? A little helper?"

Moby continued to pull at her arm, its jaws clamped hard around her sleeve. It would have drawn blood from a normal person, but Livia was not a normal person.

I didn't say anything, I wasn't goaded into feeding her bad mood. I just waited until the dog had brought her close enough.

"I made a promise," I said to Livia. "I made a promise to your mother that I'd find you. And here you are."

"Well, in future, I think you should consider whether the person you're looking for actually wants to be found."

"So, you preferred it at the bottom of a hole in the street?"

Livia laughed. "Yes, of course I did. Why wouldn't I prefer it? It was safe. I like safe."

Her words surprised me. It sounded like something I'd say, and the sudden connection to the demon felt unnerving. Livia had found her own safe spot, far below the surface of the Earth, and I felt guilty for dragging her away from it.

"I had no choice. I'm looking for someone, and your mother said she'd help."

"Well, more fool you," Livia said. "I don't think she's about to help anyone."

Moby dragged Livia until she was away from the lip of the crater, and then let go. Livia tried to run back, but she was fixed to the spot, like her mother had been before I'd taken the tennis racquet to her.

"Ah, there you are," Livia's mother said from behind us.

Both Sophia and I turned. Livia's mother was floating a little off the ground, garbed in white.

"I did what you asked, now I need to know where Freya is."

"Freya?" Livia laughed. "You want to know about Freya?"

I spun back round to Livia. "You know who she is?"

"Of course," she said. "Don't we, mother?"

"Yes, but that's enough of that. We don't share secrets, do we Livia?"

"No. Of course we don't," Livia replied.

"Wait a minute," Sophia said. "You promised you'd help Sammel. You have to help him."

"I don't have to do any such thing," Livia's mother said. "And pardon you for talking. Now, if you don't mind, we have people to upset."

"No," I said. "No, you can't."

"I can, Sammel. Who do you think you are, exactly? You're only a human. A little mortal fool. You are nothing to us."

"I hurt you before, with the racquet."

"In your mind," Livia's mother said. "But nothing more."

Livia's mother turned to leave. She floated about a metre before stopping.

"No, you don't," came a deep voice from out of thin air.

Livia's mother spun round. Her body language changed. She was frightened. "No, not you!"

"It's been a long time," Akono said. I looked around but couldn't see him. Then I realised everyone was looking at me. Akono's voice was coming out of me.

"You made a promise to this boy," Akono said. "You must keep it."

"You won't harm me," Livia's mother said. "You're nothing."

"Very well," the ghost replied.

I felt him – me – breathe in, a sudden, far-too-quick-to-be-real breath. Livia's mother screamed. Something came away from her, some part of her, and entered my mouth. I could taste it, too. It tasted of... pity.

Livia's mother fell to the floor.

"No!" screamed Livia. I turned and saw her run to her mother. "No, you can't do it."

"I will take her piece by piece. Until she is no more."

"Then I will tell you," Livia said. "I will tell you about Freya."

"No, Livia," Livia's mother said, weakly. "You mustn't. You mustn't give them what they want."

"I won't let them harm you."

"If you tell them, you are... a bigger fool... than I thought you were."

Livia looked at me with fear. Whoever Akono was, he took no prisoners.

"Go to the beach," Livia said. "Go to the beach and find Freya there."

"Which beach?" Sophia asked.

"Sammel knows," she replied. "Sammel has always known."

"Leave this man alone," Akono replied. "Never find him again, or I will be waiting."

Livia hissed then, like a cat. She spat, too. Something black on the ground. Then she took her mother's hand, and they were gone, evaporated into a fine mist.

"Thank you," I said to Akono.

"On the contrary. I've been waiting for the chance to deal with her. I took more than she'll ever realise. Good day, Sammel."

"Good day, Akono."

With that, the ghost was gone. I looked around for Moby, but it was gone, too. For a moment, I wondered if Moby and Akono might have been the same.

"I think we ought to find somewhere to sleep," Sophia said.

And we walked back to the car, alone.

*

We parked by a hotel just out of town. It sat on a junction of the main road; a spider awaiting its weary customers. They had a cheap room with two single beds, which suited us. We settled in and ordered room service, just a couple of burgers and fries.

When they arrived, we opened the doors to the small balcony and sat out there, eating.

"So, there's a beach somewhere?" Sophia asked.

"Must be," I said. "But I can't remember where or what it looks like."

"Still, the information's in there," she said, tapping my temple, lightly. "We just need to get it out."

"I don't know how to do that."

We looked down on the junction. It had grown quiet.

"I've been thinking," Sophia said. "When you came into the café, when I first saw you, you were talking to someone. Who was that?"

I smiled. "I didn't think you'd noticed."

"I'm a writer. I notice a lot."

"That was Bobby. I mentioned him?"

"I remember. Well, perhaps we can get him here now."

"We left him at the pub, remember?"

Sophia looked at me. "Ah," she said. "I wondered whether you were aware."

I blinked. "Aware of what?"

"Well, you know I couldn't see Moby at first?"

"Yes."

"In the café, I saw you talking, but there wasn't anyone sitting opposite you."

"No," I said to her. "That can't be. Bobby's real. He's always been real. A real person, like you and me."

"Yes, *we're* real, Sammel, but I don't think Bobby is."

I sat there in silence for a moment.

"She's a fucking *keeper*," Bobby said from somewhere inside the room.

I almost fell off my chair. "Bobby?" I asked.

"The one and fucking only," he replied. Slowly, he appeared from the shadows, a big, shit-eating grin on his face.

*

"You still can't see him?" I asked Sophia.

She shook her head. "Nope. No one there."

I looked at Bobby. He sat on the floor by the open doors. I reached out and tried to touch him, but my hand went straight through.

"So, you're not even a demon," I said.

"Not a demon. Of course I'm not a demon. Fucking scum."

"Then what are you?"

"Ask her," he said, nodding in the direction of Sophia. "She's smart."

I looked at Sophia. "He said to ask you who he is."

"I think," Sophia said. "I think Bobby represents the part of you that you suppress. Someone who can say and do the things you can't."

"I've made him up?"

"Perhaps, but he's as real to you as I am."

I turned to Bobby. "That's true?" Bobby nodded.

"Sure is. I'm you. You're me."

"But you text me?"

"You really think there's any-fucking-thing on your phone from me?"

"But why would I make you up?"

"I don't know," Bobby said. "What I do know, what I do remember, is the day you created me. And you're not going to fucking believe this, but it was on a beach."

I felt electricity flow down my spine. Everything was connected, and now I was seeing some of it.

"He says the day he was created I was on a beach."

"Ask him which one."

Bobby put his hand up. "Yeah, I heard her," he said, with a smile. "But you ain't getting it that easily. We'll go there tomorrow. I'll guide you, capiche?"

"Capiche," I agreed. "He's going to take us there tomorrow," I told Sophia.

"That sounds like progress," she replied.

Bobby went then, leaving us in peace. I felt odd. Part of me must have known he was never real, but another part relied on him so much that I wasn't sure how I could continue with this new knowledge. Sophia opened a bottle of wine and poured it into two plastic cups she'd produced from her bag. Before I'd had a chance to raise it to my lips, she lifted her cup high into the air.

"A toast," Sophia said.

"A toast," I repeated.

"To Bobby," she said. "A good friend."

"To Bobby," I replied. "A fucking good friend." I blushed slightly, but Sophia laughed and made everything okay.

We went through the motions of clinking the cups, but no clinking sound was made. We sipped, we watched and we listened to the sounds of the night as it grew darker around us.

"What happens when I learn all the secrets?" I asked Sophia.

"You never will, Sammel," she told me. "No one ever knows all the secrets."

*

The next morning, we woke, dressed, and walked across the road to the fast food restaurant opposite. The food was as expected, which was fine. Safe, almost.

We returned to the hotel and loaded up the car with our belongings.

"Still no sign of Bobby?" Sophia asked.

I shook my head.

"He'll turn up when he's ready."

We stopped for petrol a little way down the road, and I went to use the bathroom. Bobby was already in there, using a urinal.

"I really don't understand how my mind works," I said when I saw him.

"And a happy fucking morning to you."

*

"So where are we heading?" Sophia asked, after I'd told her I'd found Bobby.

"Just head to the coast, along the main road," he said, pointing in a general direction.

"He says that way."

"Then that way, it is," she said with a smile.

*

Two hours later, we turned off the main route and headed down towards the coast. The radio was quietened so I could listen to Bobby's directions.

"Pull over," he said, finally. "We're here."

"This is the place?" I asked.

"Oh, yeah," Bobby replied. "This is the place."

Sophia parked the car.

"Do you recognise it?" she asked me.

"Don't think so."

"You gotta go down there, Sammel," Bobby said from the back seat. "Go down and you'll remember. I'm sure of it."

"Bobby says I have to go down."

"On your own?"

"I think so."

Sophia leant in and kissed me on the cheek. "Be safe, Sammel," she said. "If you start feeling nervous, or not up to it, you come back, or shout for me."

"I will."

"I think you're being very brave."

*

I got out and shut the door. I'd come a long way in such a short time. Something had been triggered, something which had set me on a path to Sophia, to here.

The sky was clear now. I could feel the sun on my skin, and it made me happy. I smiled at Sophia, sitting behind the steering wheel, then walked around the front of her car and up the grassy slope to the promenade.

This beach was also made of pebbles. Many different colours and textures, spread out to make a surface I could walk upon. When I stepped on them, they shifted and made that unique sound pebbles made. Something sparked in my chest. A reaction, not a memory. A kicking sensation, which could have been fear, could have been excitement. I tried to push at it, to explore it further, but it went as soon as it had arrived.

The pebbles stretched out to the sand, and then the sand drifted under the waves. There was an order here, and I was starting to understand how things worked.

As I walked to the sea, the wet sand compacted at the edges of my shoes. Something about this made me smile in a sad way, so I just kept moving, past the seaweed and the rock pools, past everything, until I'd reached the water's edge, where I waited for the end.

There were other things waiting there, too. Waiting with me, watching as this played out. This was as important to them, as it was to me. How long had they been waiting for? Since I was last here?

I took my shoes and socks off, and threw them further up, onto the pebbles. The tide was on its way out, so I knew I had plenty of time to retrieve them when all of this was done. I moved my phone and wallet up to my top pockets, and began to wade out into the water. It wasn't as warm as I'd hoped, or as I'd dreamed in Sophia's car.

"Stop," came a girl's voice from behind me. "There's no need to go any further."

"Freya?" I asked.

"Yes, Sammel," Freya said. "Yes, you have found me, at last."

*

Something happened to time.

I was at the beach, but I didn't want to be there. My mother and father had brought me here, and now they were in the car arguing about something, and if I had to guess what the something was I'd say it was about her drinking. She always smelt of alcohol, so I always assumed she'd been drinking.

I was alone at the beach, standing on the sand in my shorts and t-shirt, wondering what it was I was supposed to do without them here.

This was the first day of the holiday. The day before my father had arrived home from work, telling us he'd managed to book some time off, and that one of his colleagues had said we could stay in their holiday home for a few days.

My mother had hated the idea, but I think she thought twice when she saw my face light up at the notion of not having to be stuck within the same four walls.

We had packed that evening, though not ever having had a holiday before, I didn't really know what I was doing, so packed five pairs of shorts, one t-shirt, a pair of pants, and three pairs of odd socks. It was all a bit of a mad rush, but by lunch the next day, we had reached the holiday home and I was eager to do whatever it was that people on holiday did.

We went to the beach for an hour, then returned and stayed in, so we could 'get acquainted' with the home, even though it seemed straightforward, even to someone as young as I was. I must admit, though, staying in was better than I'd thought. We played a couple of card games, watched some television, and even had a dessert after dinner. When I went to sleep in the spare room, I was comfy, and above all else, safe.

If this was what holidays were like, I wanted more.

*

In the morning, I woke to the strains of a conversation trying hard not to be a disagreement. Something was the matter, but as the sun shone through my new bedroom window, I was willing to ignore it. In fact, I washed, ate some toast and got dressed all by myself.

I told my parents I was going to play outside, and wouldn't go beyond sight of the house. They both agreed, I'm sure, happy in the knowledge they could now argue at full volume without having to worry about upsetting me.

*

The house, which was more like a hut, was set in a small field. All around, trees and shrubs defined a loose kind of border, and I made sure I stayed within its boundaries as I played my games of make-believe. In truth, I was just as afraid at losing my parents, as they were of losing me.

After about an hour, I grew restless and decided I'd build a fire. I ventured between the trees, picking up large twigs and small branches, making sure I could see the hut most of the time. When

I'd collected enough, I found a spot by a fallen tree, arranged what I'd collected in a loose tepee formation, then retrieved the box of matches I'd snuck out of the house. The first two matches were duds, but the third lit, and I placed it against the dry wood, making it crackle and spurt into life.

I felt proud. I had only ever watched my father set a fire in the hearth at our house. It wasn't as practised as his, but it was good enough. At first, the smoke rose in wisps, but then, as the heavier twigs began to take, it grew heavier, darker.

I sat on the floor smiling and feeding the flames. It was like bringing life into the world, and the smell of the smoke started to wash over me. It was a good smell. A satisfying smell.

*

She came from out of the flames, or at least, that's what it looked like. One moment, I was staring at the yellow tongues, wondering what it would feel like to put my hand in, and the next, something moved within their depths. I remember crying out and scuttling back, away from it.

The smoke was very thick now, and it distorted the area around me. I moved to the side to get a better view and that was the first time I saw her, standing, dressed in the green of the forest, moccasins on her feet, silk scarf around her shoulders.

"Hello," she said. I was glad she spoke first; I was completely struck dumb. "I'm Freya."

"Sammel," I croaked. I coughed, cleared my throat, and said again. "I'm Sammel."

She sat quickly, cross-legged on the ground, and smiled at me. "It's a nice fire," she said.

"Thank you. Where did you come from?"

"I live in the forest."

"In the forest? In the trees?"

Freya laughed. "No, not in the trees. We have a home there."

"Oh," I said. "Of course."

"Where are your parents?"

I nodded in the direction of the house. "In there, trying to argue with their voices down."

"Oh, dear," she said with a sigh. She seemed to mean it, too. She seemed to understand what I meant. I'm almost certain that a boy of seven cannot fall in love. Still, whatever love's young equivalent might be, I felt it then, for this girl from the forest.

"Would you like to go for a walk?" I asked. I'd become aware my parents could appear at any minute, and I didn't want them to call me away from this person.

"Yes," Freya said. "Let's walk."

*

For a while, we walked in the wood, Freya threading herself in and out with a delicate ease. I watched her all the way, and it felt like she watched me, too. Time altered, became slow and then fast, and then slow all over again. I'm not sure how long we walked for. What I am sure of, is that when at last I did lose my footing, and had to stop myself from falling, I realised I had no idea where I was.

"This way," Freya said, holding out her hand. Naturally I took it. There was nothing else in the world I wanted to do more at that moment than be connected to her. Her hand was cool, I remembered. Cool and smooth. It reminded me of marble. The fireplace at home had a marble surround, and it was like touching that.

We changed direction, turned ninety degrees to the left, and, for a moment, I wondered where we might be going. I wondered why I had left the safety of the holiday home. I wondered who I was. Then, an instant later, I became lost once more within the step of this girl.

*

After a while, we emerged through the trees, onto a grassy area, and I knew exactly where we were. The sound of the sea was off to the right, and seagulls flew overhead. We were back at the beach.

"That's where I usually play," Freya said, indicating the sand. "Would you like to build a castle with me?" I nodded. "Come on, then," she said. She let go of my hand and started running along the pebbles, heading towards the waves. It was a strange sensation; a jolt from within me. Like something had been taken away. I gasped, and my hand went to my chest. Then I ran, eyes fixed on the woodland girl.

*

She didn't look behind the whole way to the sea, and she didn't slow down, either. When I reached the pebbles, I stopped to catch my breath. Freya reached the shoreline and stood with the waves breaking over her feet, looking out to the horizon. I knew she wanted to keep going. She wanted to run into the water and come out somewhere different. She didn't want to be hemmed in by anything.

I began the slow walk down, my legs already aching from the exercise. The pebbles were hard to balance on, slipping and sliding under my young, tired legs. Then I was on the sand, walking through its softness with bare feet. I looked behind and saw I'd taken my shoes and socks off, and left them, behind me, on the stones.

"Come on," Freya called. "Come on."

I picked up the pace, I didn't want to let her down. She was holding her hand out again, and I took it, felt the coolness again. It was like holding a pebble, I thought.

We walked into the water like it was the most natural of things to do, yet there was an urgency there; she was pulling me deeper and deeper. I'd be all right, though; Freya would make everything all right.

The water reached over our hips, and was up around our stomachs when she stopped.

"Here we are," Freya said.

"Where?" I asked.

"This is the place, can't you feel it?"

I nodded, but I couldn't feel anything. Freya turned her gaze to the horizon.

"I'm so glad I found you today," she said. "I've been waiting for someone to take me here."

"Who are you?" I asked, instinctively.

"I am Freya," she said. "Do you know that feeling of loss you had, when I let go of your hand?"

"Yes."

"That's what I feel all the time."

"What for?"

"I've been stuck here all my life, Sammel Ahlberg, and whatever my appearance, I have had a very long life. I need to stretch my wings. I need to escape this place."

"Then why don't you?"

"I can't," Freya said. "I can't leave this place. Not without your help. Will you help?"

I was frightened by the question, frightened by the look in her eyes, but I was most frightened by the fact I knew I would help her. Help her leave. Whatever she asked me to do, I thought I would do.

"How?" I asked.

"You have to take my place," she said. "You have to stay here."

It was like the breath had been sucked out of me.

"I... I can't," I told her. "I have my own place to be."

"If you don't take my place, they will never stop looking for me. I will always be part of here. Please help me."

"But... I can't."

Her look of hope turned to hatred. "Then may you be cursed, Sammel Ahlberg. Cursed with unknowing. Cursed with memories always just out of reach. With the feeling of madness. With the feeling of loss."

Then she went. She fell beneath the water, and was gone.

"Freya," I called to the place where she'd stood. "Freya!"

I ducked under the water, but there was nothing to see. I was blind but for touch. I reached out, tried to feel where she had gone, but she was no longer there. My fingertips scraped the bottom of the sea bed. Nothing.

Then I touched something as smooth as her hand, and I took it and brought it above the surface. It was a stone; a black stone that had no right to be in the ocean as bleak as this. I looked at the stone. It had a hole running through it.

I looked back out to the sea, and didn't know why I was there, or how I'd got there, or where my parents were. I knew nothing. I turned and waded out of the water, back onto the beach. I fetched my shoes and put them on. I did all these things, and the feeling of madness never left me.

I climbed up the pebbles, over the grass and back through the trees. I was lost, and when I was just about to give up hope, I came upon three huts in a clearing, but I've already said about that.

*

I turned and looked at Freya. She was older now, and I recognised her.

It was Selina. The barmaid from my home town. The woman I found collapsed on the pier. The woman whose life I saved.

"Hello, Sammel," she said.

"Hello, Freya."

"Call me Selina. I like Selina now."

"I remember what happened," I told her. "I remember your curse. Your hex."

"It was a stupid thing, said by a stupid girl who didn't know better. I'm sorry, Sammel. It was a mistake."

"You lived in my town all these years?"

"I live by the sea. I could not escape it, however hard I tried. Still, I could travel within it, around the coast, living under piers as I went. Finally, I found myself a place I could stay."

"Did you know it was where I lived?"

Selina shook her head. "You weren't there then, Sammel. You came and found me."

Someone stepped onto the pebbles behind her, and I moved to see who it was.

"Jackson?"

"I told you they'd look for me, didn't I?" Selina said. "He's been trying to bring me back for a long time."

The officer made his way down the beach.

"Why didn't you just tell me who you were?" I asked Selina.

"Because I didn't want to go."

"And now you do?"

She smiled. "I've had enough of this place. Haven't you? It's time for you to leave, too."

Jackson was at the edge of the water. I stepped closer to Selina, and held out my hand. She took it.

"Still smooth," I said.

"Always."

I put my arms around her and hugged as hard as I could. "I'm sorry," I said.

"I'm sorry," Selina replied.

I stood away. "What happens now?"

"You know what happens," she replied. I nodded.

I walked out of the water, passing Jackson, who didn't look at me. I walked over the sand. I walked over the pebbles.

I put my socks and shoes on, crossed the tarmac, and returned to the car. Sophia was waiting for me.

"I remember," I told her, as I opened the car door. "I remember everything."

Sophia reached across and squeezed my hand.

"I'm pleased, Sammel," she said.

I felt safe.

Epilogue

After a little searching, we found the holiday home. It wasn't in a good state. The roof was falling in, and the steps up to the door didn't look safe to walk on. We walked on them, anyway.

"Is this Songström?" Sophia asked.

I nodded. "This is how the last hut looked. How much have I forgotten, Sophia?"

"I don't know. Let's go inside," she said. "Let's see."

The door was falling off its hinges, so we pushed it open, carefully. Most of the furnishings remained. The sofa, the kitchen counter, the toilet off to the right.

I went to the sofa and saw the cushion. The one with a train on it. The cloth was mostly black and rotten, the stuffing spilling out of it reminding me of maggots.

"Am I ever going to know what really happened?"

"Do you really want to know?" Sophia replied.

We left the hut at twilight. We left, and then I came back with the petrol Sophia had in the back of her car. I doused the house in it. Tried to leave no part untouched.

Then I took out the matches, struck one, and threw it.

I had a feeling standing there. I had a feeling that the hut was saying thank you. It had waited, and now it was ready. Sophia stood by me watching, and as the heat flowed over us, I imagined us inside the hut, imagined the flames catching our clothing, cleansing us along with it.

When it was gone, Sophia put her hand in mine. It was cool and smooth.

"I have a place we should go," she whispered. "I have a house that needs us. Come with me?"

And so, we left.

Printed in Great Britain
by Amazon

66644373R20156